FIGHTING FOR AIR

A Cal Meredith Mystery

by
Marsha Mildon

New Victoria Publishers

Published by New Victoria Publishers Inc., a feminist, literary, and cultural organization, PO Box 27, Norwich, VT 05055-0027.

Cover art by Ginger Brown

Printed and Bound in the USA
1 2 3 4 5 6 1999 1998 1997 1996 1995

Author's Note

There is a city called Victoria on the south end of Vancouver Island, and there are
Gulf Islands nearby—though none named Anemone. I have used these land-
scapes, but have altered them as necessary for the story. The characters and
events are solely creatures of my imagination.

Acknowledgments

Many people have helped me as I wrote this novel; some with specific comments
or information and some with moral support. In particular, I want to thank
Colleen, my best reader always, and all of the Victoria women who have
supported me over the past few years.

Library of Congress Cataloging-in-Publication Data

Mildon, Marsha, 1946—
    Fighting for air : a Cal Meredith mystery / by Marsha Mildon
        p.   cm.
    ISBN 0-934678-69-3
    1. Women detectives- -British Columbia- -Fiction. 2. Lesbians--British
Columbia- -fiction. I Title.
PR9199.3.M4565F54   1995
813' .54 --dc20   95-19144
                                                                     CIP

For Kate

Chapter One

I was the first to spot Tekla as we snorkeled toward shore. I was the first to reach shore as well. I had to escape from that menacing ocean. Besides I wanted to be the first to talk to Ginny.

We had been scuba diving in the cold lush kelp jungle of the Pacific Northwest when we lost him. Now I was standing with Ginny, watching, trying not to think, as Jay towed Tekla to shore, stopping at every five count to give him artificial respiration. I noticed that both Ginny and I were breathing in time with the AR. I also noticed we were both trembling. Ginny wasn't even aware that I was dripping all over her as she leaned against me. A mere five feet tall in sandals, she barely came up to my breasts. At five foot, eleven inches and one hundred and ninety-five pounds, I'm usually a good bet for leaning on.

"It was only a minute or so from the time Nazki noticed him missing until I saw him on the bottom," I told her, hoping this would sound reassuring, but my voice broke on *missing* and I could hardly choke out the rest. So much for being the stalwart detective who could be leaned on in any emergency.

I caught myself running my fingers through my short dark brown hair, pulling on it as if I could somehow relieve the pressure. It's an old gesture of mine; I've done it since childhood and can't seem to stop when I'm stressed. I certainly was stressed. My mind wasn't functioning, no more than two or three synapses firing, I could tell. I felt as though a thick-walled Plexiglass jar had slipped over me. This couldn't be happening. As I stood there, it seemed that Jay was swimming across the same dark patch of water, over and over, coming no closer. This must be a nightmare.

My mind couldn't face the horror and slipped away to the day before when despite my own fears I had taken an active part in the first day of this open water dive certification weekend. I had appointed myself chief photographer and tried, not entirely successfully, to gather the seven students and one instructor into the kind of compact, smiling group favored by my 85mm Nikon lens.

"Pull in a little closer there, Peter," I urged, laughing. "Janeen won't mind a hug."

My friend, and diving buddy for this weekend, Janeen, was a flamboyant redhead, extravagant in her size, her actions, and her generosity. She was also old enough to be twenty-one year-old Peter's mother. I rather enjoyed seeing him edge closer to her. Peter was Janeen's polar opposite: skinny, uptight, and extravagant only about his fanatic devotion to the welfare of dolphins. An angry young man who preferred marine mammals to his fellow humans.

"Jay, you have to be in the center front," instructed Danielle, using her Grade Seven teacher's voice. "You are the instructor."

"I'm also taller than everyone else except Tekla," Jay laughed. "We're fine as is. Let's get this taken and get on with the dive."

"Sally, you've got to be in the front row. You're almost hidden behind Nazki," I said.

"Good. I hate photographs."

"But this is the 'Before' picture, showing you while you're all still land-bound. After you complete your dives, I'll take the 'After', of seven new sea-worthy divers. So come on, everybody, best face forward. One, two, three, smile."

Just as I pressed the shutter, Mrs. Dale, Ginny Dale's mother came tottering across the road to the shoreline in her open toe heels. "Wait. Ralph and I should be in the picture too, with Virginia. We did pay for her scuba course, after all." Caroline and Ralph Dale had come along this weekend as uninvited guests, or rather chaperones for Ginny. I couldn't believe how they stuck to their daughter, rather like a pair of unpleasant limpet snails—impossible to pry off.

"Hurry up, folks. We have to do two dives today, remember. And I want them to be fun, not just a race to get finished," Jay said.

"Quick then, one more with the Dales," I agreed to get it over with. "Smile everyone. One, two, three, click."

I screwed my camera off my tripod while Jay led her students down to the shoreline. I could hear her giving instructions about the entry—an easy walk-in over fairly flat rocks—and about the skill drills they were going to do on the dive. I wasn't a student, but was only along to buddy with Janeen—Jan had insisted to me that she was terribly nervous and wouldn't do her certification if I didn't come with her. I knew this was nonsense. Jan was nervous of nothing, but I allowed myself to be convinced. I think Jay and Janeen had planned this to get me back into diving, and back in the city, it had seemed like a reasonable idea. This wasn't my first dive, only my first in ten months, five days, and three hours—not allowing for time zone changes—since my lover and partner of eight years had died, drowned in that fluke, unreasonable collapse of the shipwreck we'd been exploring off Cayman Brac. When Liz died, I'd sworn I'd never dive again, maybe never look at an ocean. And I was terrified right now. This was a stupid idea. I shouldn't be here and I shouldn't be diving.

I moved off to the side and began taking candid shots of the divers preparing. Up here in the waters off Canada's Gulf

Islands, getting suited up for diving is a major production. First, divers must don their wet suits, two-piece skin-tight straightjackets that measure at least three quarters of an inch thick over the torso. Once inside, a person can barely bend her joints, so those who can afford them wear the more comfortable and warmer drysuits donned over sweat suits or 'woolly bear' jump suits. Of course, zippered in and inflated in the drysuits, divers look like 'Michelin' women. Then the average diver adds fourteen to forty pounds of lead on a weight belt, depending on her weight and the type of suit; a forty pound tank with a buoyancy compensator vest like a life jacket that eliminates the possibility of a streamlined look; fins that make it impossible to walk forward; a mask that cuts off all but tunnel vision; and a hood and neoprene gloves so thick the sense of touch disappears. What a swell sport! It takes twenty minutes of hard labor for a skilled diver to suit up and can take an hour or more for the first time student. But the grace of movement through the water along with the wonderful creatures more than makes up for the ungainly 'on-land' part of a dive, or so I'd always believed before Liz....

"Tanks and regulators are in the van," called Jay. "Bring out two tanks for everyone and then bring a few more just in case an O-ring blows or something, we can get a new one quickly. Get suited up as fast as you can. But remember to pace yourselves with your buddy. It's only seventy degrees Fahrenheit, but the sun's strong, so you could get overheated in those suits. If you feel yourself getting hot, go sit in the ocean for a few minutes."

The dive site turned into pandemonium. Divers laid out their bright colored tarps this way and that as protection for their dive gear and the dry clothes they intended to come back to. Some hauled the tanks and regulators from Jay's van to a flat rock area, while others just as quickly grabbed them and began to gear up. I noticed that, as always, Tekla and Peter were carrying many more tanks than their share while

Ginny avoided carrying any. I supposed it was because they were both courting her. They'd almost bump into each other at the van in their eagerness to get a tank, glare at each other, then race the tank over to the rocks. I shook my head to get rid of an uninvited vision of them both with large antlers, crashing into each other, the sounds echoing through the forest. Young love, how sweet! I continued wandering about the site, clicking pictures randomly and quickly, trying to capture the sense of tension along with excitement that always precedes students' first dive. I was ignoring the fact that I should be suiting up too.

Tekla had won Ginny as his dive partner, and they had somehow grabbed the most comfortable corner of the rocky beach to suit up on. They made a handsome couple. Ginny's parents had bought her a beautiful teal and silver dry suit. I guessed they'd hoped she would meet some suitable young man in the dive class since most scuba classes are notorious for having at least a two to one ratio of men to women. Unfortunately for Ginny's parents, she had settled her fancy on Tekla. They didn't seem at all pleased with that, in fact their behavior made me think they were throwbacks to the bad times of the 'Guess Who's Coming to Dinner' era.

The rest of the students all were pulling on rental wet suits—generic black. I clicked more photos, laughing to myself, as the guys pulled on panty-hose to help them slide into the neoprene suits more easily. Nazki pranced about, apparently enjoying the humor in "his first pair of Hanes", but I could see that Tekla felt uncomfortable and tugged on his Farmer John as quickly as possible, then zipped on his jacket instantly. As Jay had predicted his rushing heated him up, and abruptly, he stormed off into the ocean, sweat pouring down his forehead.

"Watch it," shouted Dani as Tekla's splashing threatened to inundate the dry clothes she'd just laid out on her tarp.

"Watch it yourself," said Tekla. He clambered back out again and deliberately flicked water at Sally, Dani's partner.

She flinched as if hit, and turned abruptly away. "If you play by the water, you're going to get wet," he sneered, heading back to help Ginny on with her blue aluminum rental tank. Jay had told me once that she made sure her rental equipment was new every three years, basic level, and identical so that all students would have the same first experience on their dive and there'd be no question of favoritism in the rentals. Then those who were thinking of buying their own personal equipment could test fancier stuff if they wanted, but have a good base for comparison. It seemed to me that this would not help her market the most expensive equipment, but I was sure it helped students trust that they were getting value for their money.

I turned my camera's attention to Dani and Sally. I'd known Dani since high school. In fact, she'd been the one—after sharing a bottle of Baby Duck, a sweet bubbly Canadian wine of ill repute—who had confessed on her fifteenth birthday that she thought she was a lesbian. I don't remember ever being so scared or so relieved all at one time as I was when I listened to her slurring out her feelings. There was someone like me after all—only braver. It turned out that we were both 'in love' with our basketball coach, Miss Davidoff, who was remarkably resistant to our charms. So, we leaned on each other through the rest of high school as we carefully explored our discovery, and though (or perhaps because) we never had a sexual relationship, we continued to be best friends through the past twenty years.

"You and that wretched camera are being over-exposed," called Sally. Her voice was joking, but there was an irritated edge to it.

Sally and Dani had met at an Amnesty International meeting six months ago and had been inseparable ever since. I did my best to like my old friend's new lover. Sally was a medical doctor and, Dani told me, a passionate supporter of third world causes. She seemed to have a good sense of humor and tons of energy for the causes and people she cared about. Besides, she drove a classic white 1953 Jaguar XK 120 convertible that made me drool with envy since classic British sports cars are a passion of mine. But she always seemed on edge, at least at the scuba class parties I'd attended, a hair trigger away from exploding, though I had to admit she never did, not while I was around. Still, I wondered how Dani was dealing with such constant tension.

"Good point." Jay had come up behind me. "Sally, Dani, you're almost ready, way ahead of these others, so when you've done your buddy checks, just slip into the water by my float flag, inflate your buoyancy compensators, and float there doing some slow deep breathing—almost meditate. I want you very calm for the dive."

She turned her large blue eyes on me then and stared sternly. "As for you, Cal, it's time to stop stalling."

My knees got rubbery as she spoke and I sat down abruptly on the rocks. "I can't. I thought I could, but I just can't."

Jay's voice was kind when she spoke again, but I could hear the iron in it. "I understand that seeing Liz die like that was unspeakably horrible, Cal. But it wasn't your fault. There was nothing you could have done. And you've got to go on from that. Starting to dive is necessary in your healing."

"You do not understand, damn it," I forced myself not to scream at her. "No one can understand. There was no one within miles of where we'd dived. Even if I'd swum to shore, it would have taken hours to get equipment to lift the beams that had fallen on her. Even if I'd left her my tank, she couldn't have moved to change regulators. The only thing I could do was stay with her while she drowned. Have you ever watched someone drown?" I could feel tears welling up in my eyes, and started to scramble up. I had to get away from here.

Jay caught me and pulled me back down. Her long fingers clamped around my wrist. "You are going to dive today, Cal. If you want, I'll take you alone, after the class. But

I believe it's important that you face this through. Now. It's not the ocean, the water, the equipment, or you that's the problem. It was an evil fate that caught her, and I do feel the horror you felt. But you have to get past it, otherwise you'll never get on with your own life. Liz would want you to live again."

I hated knowing she was right. I had lapsed into a kind of emotional coma for the past ten months, and I had to admit I was showing no signs of coming out of it. My whole body seemed to clench into a giant knot when I even looked at the ocean. How could I possibly...?

"You have a choice," Jay said. "You can dive with us now, buddying with Janeen. You know she's been looking forward to that. Or you can wait and I'll take you later. Which will it be?"

Somehow her matter-of fact insistence helped. I took a deep breath and muttered, "Now."

"Good. I'll help you get ready," Jay said and pulled me up.

Despite my misgivings, I enjoyed the dive. After the first few minutes, I got my buoyancy exactly right and remembered the astonishing feeling of freedom that water allows, like weightlessness on the moon. I even tried a couple of somersaults. Then, while the others were practicing taking off their masks and replacing them, I found myself surrounded by a school of China Rockfish, their black and yellow markings flashing through the greeny-brown light of the kelp forest. I hovered with them just above the circle of students and let myself be enchanted by the perfection of these fish in their environment. Once again, I felt grateful to be allowed to enter as a guest. And when Jay spotted a little harbor seal, and it came to investigate us, I actually forgot Liz for a few minutes. I was disappointed when Tekla swam up and indicated to Jay that he was running low on air, so we all had to surface. Men, I thought to myself disgustedly, they always think they're such great athletes, but in an environment where slow movement and restraint are pluses, they breathe up their air, sometimes twice as fast as women. And Tekla seemed to use up his air particularly quickly.

The afternoon dive went well too. The students—all but Ginny—did their skill exercises well and quickly. Unfortunately for Ginny, her ears pained her and wouldn't equalize while we were descending, so Jay had to take her back to shore. After the dive, Sally took one look in her left ear and declared it infected, effectively eliminating Ginny's opportunity to dive for the rest of the weekend.

* * *

"It wouldn't have happened if I'd been there," Ginny shrieked, jolting me back to the present. She tore herself loose from my arm and hurled herself into the water as Jay hauled Tekla into shore. "I should have been there. Why didn't I go on the dive?" she screamed.

I meant to go after her, but I couldn't move. My feet had taken root in the sandy gravel of the island beach. My head started to float toward the group huddled around Tekla. Tall, lean Danielle caught me as I fell.

"Sit down, Cal," said Dani quietly. I sat as directed. It felt good to be closer to the ground even though part of me, a very distant part, was worried about getting grit all over my wet suit.

"We'll deal with things," Dani continued.

"Dani, get over here and get Jay out of her suit," shouted Sally, taking command like the good doctor she was.

"I've gotta do CPR," said Jay, not missing a beat as she rhythmically compressed his chest and continued inflating his lungs.

"I'll take care of that," said Sally. "You've done great, but you need to rest now. You're exhausted." She gently pushed Jay out of the way, pulled off Tekla's tank, unzipped his suit, and began compressions. "Dani, get a blanket around her. Nazki, get the resuscitator. Peter, for goodness sake, take

Ginny out of the way. She's getting hysterical. Everybody else just stand back."

"Has anyone gone to phone an ambulance?" Dani asked me as she ran past, her arms full of sleeping bags.

Her question was answered by the sound of sirens as the two Mounties that made up Anemone Island's police force and the sole ambulance sped around the last bend in the road. I had sent Janeen racing to call from my cellular in the Mini as soon as we reached shore.

The police and ambulance attendants worked quickly. One took over CPR. The other asked Danielle and Sally to take the now hysterical Ginny to the hospital. Corporal Hansen, senior Mountie on the island, took Jay to his car. He appeared to be trying to question her, but it didn't look like Jay had much to say. She was probably in shock, I thought.

I took a deep breath and tried standing up again. Ah, it was possible. I could move. I knew I'd brought a thermos of Faith's personal brand of hot chocolate, but it took what felt like hours to fumble in my dive bag and find it. After a hefty swig, I headed to the police car.

"Cal-li-o-pe Meredith," drawled Hansen, stretching out the syllables in my awkward name as if to remind himself, painfully, that we'd met before. "I might have known it would be you in the centre of trouble." He'd been a real fan of mine ever since Liz and I had broken open an adoption scandal that had been operating under his nose. He'd received an official reprimand because of that case and, ever since, gave me trouble when I came to the island. "You're the one who located the body, am I right?"

I nodded as I poured some cocoa and handed it to Jay. She gave a quick smile of thanks, then lapsed into stillness. "We were all snorkeling into shore like Jay told us."

"Jay?"

"Jennifer," I gestured at her. "She was doing open water certification dives for the new divers."

"Carry on."

"Well, I was leading at that point. All of a sudden, there he was."

"What do you mean, there he was? Exactly what did you see?"

"I saw Tekla, just like he'd looked all weekend, black wet suit, green fins. He was in about twenty feet of water, perfectly clear, and he wasn't moving, face down."

"Anything else?"

"There were no bubbles coming out of his regulator so I knew he wasn't breathing, and I could see his mask was gone. We signaled Jay right away."

"Yeah. So, tell me what happened during the dive."

I'd been trying to figure that out ever since Tekla disappeared, but it wasn't clear. I stared out into the wispy mares' tail clouds, trying to form a mental picture of those last few minutes before we'd realized Tekla was gone. "It was the third dive of the certification. I just came along this weekend," my voice broke again. How could I say it? I had come to try to exorcise the nightmares, not find more. "I came to buddy with Janeen," I choked out, "and get back into diving. It's been a while."

"So it was your third dive, but first today?"

"Yes. The others had finished all their drills."

"How long did that take?"

"About forty-five minutes. We still had lots of air, so we went off on a tour. Jay knew there were some octopuses in the area, right Jay?"

She nodded. I had to fight off a growing desire to behave like a knight-errant and whisk her away from Hansen's inquiries.

"Just tell me what you saw. I'll have plenty of time to hear her story," said Hansen.

"We were just swimming alongside a rocky drop-off, shining our lights into little crevices to see what was there."

"How deep did you go?"

"About sixty feet. That's where the most life is in these

waters."

Hansen scrawled a note in his small black notebook. "Now, tell me where you all were in relation to each other."

"It's a bit hard to say. The visibility wasn't great."

"What do you mean? How far were you from one another?"

"I'm not sure, maybe ten—fifteen feet."

"Are you kidding?" Hansen exploded. "I've done some diving, you know. And seen people a hundred feet away."

"Sure, and you've been diving in the Caribbean, right?"

"So?"

"So, because of the mixing of the cold and warm currents here, we have an incredible amount of plankton. That's good because it feeds the whales and a lot of other life. But it's bad because it cuts the visibility."

"You mean you don't see more than ten or fifteen feet on a dive?"

"Yeah, we do. But there's a lot of clay silt here from the mouth of the river. It covers the rocks, and you kick up clouds of the stuff if you drag your fins in it. The new students cloud it up pretty thoroughly. Anyhow, Janeen and I were following Jay and Peter, though we were mostly trying to tickle the ling cod—they just sit there looking dumb until you touch them."

"The people, Meredith, not the fish."

"Hey, I was watching the fish." I glanced back at Jay. She was shivering. "Can we take her someplace warm?"

"If it's so damn cold down there, Meredith, how come your instructor's wearing a dry suit, but she lets you all dive in wet suits?"

"That's normal. Instructors spend a lot of time in the water doing nothing but watching students. They get frozen while the students work on the drills. It's quite comfortable in the wet suits when you're moving all the time, but I don't know any instructors who wear wet suits in these waters anymore."

"Wouldn't catch me diving up here in a wet suit," Hansen

grimaced. It was funny to see his six foot two frame shivering at the very thought of our beautiful Pacific. "So who the hell could you see down there, Meredith?"

"Jay had us arranged in the typical instructor's box. Peter was buddying with her. We were a bit behind and to her left. Danielle and Sally were over to our right, though I could only see silt clouds in their direction. Sally didn't seem to have a lot of co-ordination and kept stirring up the muck. Nazki and Tekla were centered behind us, or I thought they were."

"But you could only see the instructor and Peter, right?"

"I was only watching for them."

"Why was she buddying with a student?"

"One of the others dropped out leaving an uneven number. Peter was an amazingly good diver for a beginner so I think she wanted him with her because he wouldn't need all her attention. Besides, he didn't get along too well with some of the others."

"Then what happened?"

"Jay and Peter turned to the left and we followed. Jay had spotted an octopus and lured it out of its cave. They're beautiful animals, you know." I always try to do a commercial for octopuses. They are gentle shy creatures with an incredibly bad rep. "This one turned pale, almost white at first. They do that when they're disturbed. But Jay's so good with the life, she just held out her hand and it settled there and relaxed and developed some reddish stripes. Then it spread out its tentacles and the two of them started dancing. Pure ballet."

"The divers," Hansen growled.

"We were all watching Jay and the octopus, sort of mesmerized, when Nazki swam up to Jay and started motioning frantically."

"And?"

"We surfaced. Nazki said Tekla had disappeared and Jay told me to lead the others into shore on the surface. She was scanning the surface for bubbles, but when she didn't see any, she dived back down to look for him."

"And that's when you saw him?"

"After we'd been swimming one or two minutes. He was maybe fifty yards toward the shore from where we surfaced."

"Did you see anything at all that would help you understand what happened? Anything around where he was?"

I hesitated.

"Come on, I need your help here. I don't like accidents on my turf," he said.

"Only an odd thing. He had one glove off. We found it later, floating into shore. We never did find his mask."

"How would he lose a mask?"

"Haven't you ever had your buddy kick your mask? Or a large fish? Seals like to bump at them, and an octopus could pull one off, but it's unlikely. Or he could have taken it off, in a panic."

"And why would he take off a glove?"

"I have no idea. The rental gloves like he had can be darned near impossible to get off, even on land."

"Thanks," said Hansen. "You've got a good eye for detail."

"Why thank you, Corporal," I said. "I know we little old private investigators don't have the abilities of you *real* police, but—"

Hansen got out of the squad car abruptly and motioned for me to come with him. We walked to the shore and stared out over the sea. It was a mirror-smooth indigo, unusual for Easter time in the Pacific Northwest, reflecting the sun now so brightly I squinted, even through my hundred percent UV protected sunglasses. The mountains on the mainland reared up looking close enough to touch. What a vista. I knew Jay liked to train her students here, partly because there was so much life down below at easy dive sites, but also because of the beauty. And she thought the weekend of camaraderie away from the city was an extra bonus she could give her students. How could that have gone so wrong? The thick jar slipped over me again. Numbness returned. Nothing awful could have happened here. It was just another of those night-mares, since Liz....

"One more question," Hansen said. "As you followed your instructor, how often did you see her turning around and checking where you all were during this tour?"

I stared into the sky again. "I can't say for sure. A lot of the time, I could only see her fins."

"So you couldn't see her looking at all?"

"I didn't say that. She wears a fluorescent pink mask and I saw it, but I couldn't tell you how often."

"If you couldn't see her, how could she see you?"

"She knows what to look for."

"Thanks," Hansen said, making more notes. Then he strode back to his car and called the other divers together. "I don't know what's going to happen at the hospital," he announced. "But the young man had no pulse when they took him. I'll need to get statements from all of you today before you leave the island. Constable Groves will give you each an appointment to meet me down at our office later. Meantime, you should go get something hot in your stom-achs. None of you looks very good."

The others dispersed so quickly it was as if devils were chasing them. Only Sally thought to start hauling all the tanks and regs back into Jay's van, then Dani and Jan helped her finish. I sat watching them, a small part of my mind thinking I should help, but most of me feeling totally exhausted, unable to imagine ever moving again.

Chapter Two

"Name?"

I leaned back against the plastic emergency room chair as if I could somehow remove myself from the entire experience. Janeen had driven us in my Mini straight from the beach to the hospital, and now we were trying to get information about Tekla's condition. Instead we were giving it. Thank goodness Jan was dealing with the inquisitor. After seventeen years as a mother, eleven of them divorced and struggling to support three boys, she could handle almost anything. I wasn't sure I could speak coherently at this point.

"Tekla Takale," said Janeen. "He's Ethiopian."

"Age?" asked the nurse.

"Around twenty-five or thirty, I guess. He's doing his doctorate in economics at the University of Victoria."

"Next of kin?"

Janeen sighed. "I don't really know. I heard he was related to Haile Selassie, the old Emperor of Ethiopia, but I guess that's not much help."

"Can you identify this?"

I heard Jan mumble something, then she came over and showed me a small stone with a rough sketch of an eye painted across it in red. Apparently, Tekla had been clutching this in his bare hand. Neither Jan nor I had seen it before so couldn't help.

The rest of the dive class drifted in, except for Ginny, who'd been given a tranquilizer and a place to lie down. I watched carefully, trying to remember every single detail I knew about them, and to file each detail in separate, retrievable, brain wrinkles. I have a rather unscientific but immediate relationship with my brain. When I'm desperate to think of something, I can imagine—no, I can feel—a tiny stylus running up and down the grooves of my brain, forcing the synapses to send out their little signals. I always know where the information comes from; I swear I can feel my brain itch. But just then, I was trying to avoid the millions of brain wrinkles devoted to Liz, especially those first minutes at the wreck when I'd struggled to shift the debris.

I'd known Jay for five years, ever since Liz had convinced me that we absolutely had to learn to scuba dive. After Liz died, Jay had seemed to consider it her duty to keep me cheerful. She and Janeen had regaled me with stories of what a great scuba class this was, then nagged me into coming to all of their monthly pizza and pool dive sessions.

That was when I'd first met Tekla. He was tall, slim, and very dark. A quiet, even ascetic young man, he never indulged in the junk food and beer at the parties, but occasionally let go with a wicked joke that told of a razor wit and observant mind behind his closed expression. Most of the time, he was silent or spoke single-mindedly of his plans to change the face of third world countries. Of course, he also spent a lot of time with his arm around Ginny, ruffling her curly blonde hair or smooching with her in a corner. They made a striking couple on a dance floor, magically sensing each other's movements, creating private jazz ballets.

Nazki Kiflu, the other Ethiopian student and Tekla's constant companion, was the exact opposite. Short and Semitic looking, he was always the life of the parties; dancing with everyone or by himself when the rest of us were tired. He could spin stories for hours of his explorations around the landscape of his childhood home in Massawa, making the corals of the Red Sea come alive right in Jay's living room. He talked of his boyhood days, skin diving with no equipment to catch crabs for the family dinner table. His tales of discovering British culture when he and Tekla studied together at the London School of Economics, and the pranks he pulled on the staid Londoners, were even more diverting. Nazki acted as if it was his role in life to make anyone who passed his way feel a bit happier.

He wasn't entertaining anyone right now though. He was leaning against the waiting room wall, ever present Blue Jays baseball cap pushed back on his head, guzzling a litre bottle of Coke he'd found somewhere. True, he was uncharacteristically silent, but he looked oddly as if he were watching some distant ball game, rather than waiting in an emergency room to see if his friend had drowned.

Both Tekla and Nazki were studying third-world economics and were well into their doctorates. I always had a vision of them heading up UN conferences on development ten years down the road, convincing us fat cats to give up fifty percent or more of our wealth. They could do it. Despite their differences in temperament, I'd heard them both talk charismatically about radical answers to north-south problems. But what would happen if Tekla died, I wondered? How would that affect Nazki?

Dani and Sally had come into the waiting room arm in arm, but as was often the case with them, they did not look much like a couple. Dani sat immediately in an upright wooden chair, looking serious but totally relaxed and comfortable somehow. Sally, on the other hand, was pacing the perimeter of the room as if it were a lion's cage. Perhaps doctors aren't comfortable in hospital waiting rooms.

I had always thought they made an odd looking couple. Dani was long, lean, and angular, with blue eyes shortsighted almost to blindness. Without her glasses, she looked a lot like a giant, but lost, baby bird, although as I recall from basketball, she had a devastatingly accurate shot. Sally, on the other hand, was no more than five foot three inches, but crackling with energy, and sporting a spiked blonde hair cut so thick that strangers would reach out impulsively to pat it. She always looked about nineteen, about as unlike a serious medical doctor as I could imagine. And, if the number of times she came home with bruises and bumps was any indication, she was magnificently uncoordinated and unathletic.

They were heading for Guatemala together in another two months as part of a feminist international aid group. I had always admired the unflagging optimism with which Dani approached her charges in the inner city public school where she taught. But I knew she felt pressure to stay closeted in the school system and that took an incredible toll on her. So I was glad about the third world opportunity that had come up even though I'd miss her cheery courageous presence. She'd been recruited to teach Mayan school teachers at a college in the rain forest in Guatemala. Sally had been hired by a nearby women's health co-operative. They intended to scuba dive through the whole of the Caribbean during their time off.

Then there was Peter Demchuk, dolphin lover. He had seen his first dolphin at eleven and been determined ever since to have a career in marine biology and to save the oceans, single-handedly if necessary. In preparation, he volunteered for The Dolphin Project, our local ocean research group, doing whatever jobs were available from licking envelopes to collecting bottles for funds. He talked of dolphins, ocean ecology, even plankton as if he had a personal relationship with them all. In fact, his enthusiasm was so all pervasive, so close to obsessive, that even though I supported his ideas, I often found him downright irritating.

My mind slipped back to the morning, really only three and a half hours ago, though it seemed like years had passed. I had suited up quite happily and quickly, then wandered around snapping more pictures as the student divers practiced using a compass on land in preparation for using one underwater. It was intriguing to see how they'd changed in their approach to suiting up from their first day to their second. Peter, who was diving with Jay today, seemed particularly pleased with himself. Perhaps he's turned his affections from Ginny to Jay, I thought as I watched him scurrying about bringing Jay a juice, fetching her tool box from the van, and generally acting the chivalrous knight. Jay, however, seemed to barely notice. In fact, she was unusually quiet even for her.

Tekla and Nazki weren't quiet. Being the first ready, they raced for the water like school boys. Nazki decided to imitate a harbor seal, throwing his legs in the air, clapping his fins together, and barking at the same time. For a minute, I thought I saw an actual seal poke his eyes and whiskers out of the water to stare quizzically at Naz, before disappearing in apparent disgust. I couldn't be certain; I saw it only for a second and at a distance, but seals are notoriously curious so I thought it had probably been there.

Tekla was amusing himself by heckling the slow pokes. At one point, I thought Pete might actually charge into the water to punch him out when Tekla made snide references to teacher's pets. Sally and Dani, on the other hand, just turned away from Tekla when he suggested they might need a man to help them get their gear on. Sally, in particular, did seem unusually clumsy this morning, even dropping her tank on the rocks at one point. For her part, Dani just looked tired, and I wondered if their sex life was taking entirely too much energy, or if they were having problems. I resolutely hoped it was the former.

Finally, we all headed into the water with Jay, and the dive began perfectly normally. Each buddy pair did a compass swim from one of Jay's floats to the other with the rest of us trailing behind. I chuckled as I watched them struggle to keep the compass perfectly level to avoid getting the needle stuck. As usual, Peter did an almost flawless exercise, but unusually, Tekla had a difficult time. He didn't seem to realize that his left leg was much stronger than his right, so he kept pushing himself off course, correcting, but then starting off again several feet to the right of where he'd begun. Consequently, he missed the second float by a wide margin and I could see he wasn't pleased with his results. I wondered if he'd be using up even more air with his irritation, but when Jay had checked everyone's air at the end of the drills, we all had enough for us to go on a tour.

* * *

"Can you tell me what's happening to him?" Janeen's voice was rising. She was never patient with bureaucracy.

"They're doing everything possible," said the clerk.

Just then, Ginny, pursued by her red-faced father, burst into the waiting room. "I don't care what you think," she shouted. "I'm going to stay right here until he's fine again."

Ralph Dale caught her by the shoulder and began to shake her. "You're coming back to Victoria now with your mother and me, Virginia, and you're never seeing that...." He halted in mid-sentence when he noticed us all watching. It had been clear all weekend that Ginny's parents, ensconced near the dive site in a thirty foot motor home, were not pleased by their daughter's association with Tekla.

Caroline Dale slipped up beside her daughter now and tentatively took her husband's hand from Ginny's shoulder. "Let her check on him, Father," she simpered. "Then she'll come along like a good girl."

I felt like throwing up. Ralph Dale was everything I despised: belligerent, bigoted, self-righteous, and violent. Little Mrs. Dale was a fluttery barbie doll of a woman who apparently spent her days anticipating Ralph's every desire, and trying to deflect his anger, especially from Ginny. Mrs. Dale's only hint of a unique existence, separate from Ralph, was that she was the one who drove the motor home, handling the thirty-foot beast like a teamster. To see her swinging that wheel around was to question all stereotypes.

According to Ginny, her uncle, who ran a trucking outfit, had raised his younger sister in the family garage, teaching her everything about vehicles and hiring her to drive eighteen-wheelers before she was 'born again' at Ralph's church and then married him. It was this uncle's motor home, and he lent it occasionally to the Dales on condition that his sister and 'not that mealy-mouthed wimp of a preacher-husband' do the driving. I could understand how he felt.

I pulled myself upright in my seat and called out to Ginny, "How're you feeling?"

Her eyes filled with tears. "They gave me some sort of shot, but I don't feel any different. I just can't believe any of this is happening." She started to sway, and Sally was up and guiding her to a chair beside me before I registered that she might faint.

"Get that woman away from my daughter. Murderer," shrieked Caroline Dale. "I've seen you going into that abortion clinic." She started toward Sally who backed away, one step at a time, but with fists clenched, obviously prepared to defend herself physically. She stopped only when she was back beside Dani, who also looked ready to do battle. The rest of us hunted for places to stare in the uncomfortable silence until Caroline returned to her husband's side.

"Virginia," Ralph Dale began again. "I don't care how much you think you like this...this foreign boy. You are coming home with your mother and me. I'll give you half an hour to straighten up, get yourself looking decent, and then your mother and I are leaving. You will be with us." He turned on his heel and marched out with Caroline trotting smugly behind him.

I continued to sit, trying to keep my mind blank, but the others kept chatting and pacing the waiting room. Finally, a nurse came briskly through the double doors toward us. "You came with the young diver?" she asked the air in front of her.

"Yes," said Janeen. "How is he? Can we see—?"

"I'm sorry. We've lost him. There never were any life signs. There'll be an autopsy in the morning."

Ginny let out an agonized scream, then ran toward the double doors the nurse had just come from. "It's not true. I have to see him." She disappeared through the doors.

"You can't go in there," shouted the nurse, seconds too late.

In a flash, Sally'd jumped up and headed after her, leaving the nurse staring. Minutes later, she reappeared, half supporting, half pushing Ginny ahead of her. I was surprised to see tears welling around Sally's eyes. I thought doctors were used to these scenes.

"He's all right." Ginny growled. Her jaw was set in a hard line, her eyes dull. "Just a couple of days and he'll be fine."

"I'll book her in here overnight," said Sally, "and see that she has no visitors. The last thing she needs is the help of those parents."

"Maybe we should stay with her," Janeen whispered to me. "After all—"

The dam broke. I knew Ginny needed help. But I couldn't. All I wanted was to be alone, far away from any of this, far away from talk about death, far from the nightmare. I started shaking from head to toe and couldn't stop it. "I can't, Jan—"

Janeen was instantly solicitous. "Sorry, Cal. I should have realized. Come on, let's get back to Faith's." She put an arm around my shoulder and headed us to the parking lot.

Chapter Three

The dive class, with the exception of Ginny, trickled back to Faith's as their police interviews were completed. Evidently Hansen wanted each person's perspective since he hadn't had an accidental death on the island for three years. I had to admit I remembered he was a thorough cop, even if his 'crime-side' manners were notoriously unpleasant. It seemed as if no one wanted to leave for the ferry trip back home to Victoria, the small city where we all lived and worked. A city of Tudor pubs, Dickensian tea houses, and clouds of spring cherry blossoms, Victoria is a dreamy little back water on Vancouver Island, far from the industrial pace of larger Canadian cities. Senior citizens, year-round gardeners, and the few of us who can actually find work there love our tea-cozy lifestyle, though it means we aren't quite a part of the late twentieth century. But that evening, no one wanted Victoria. It was as if the act of leaving Anemone, normally a magical holiday island, would somehow give reality to the day's horrid events.

I didn't stay long downstairs with the others to be polite, but went to lie down in the tower room, the room where I always stayed when I visited Faith. I'd met Faith, when she was a mere sixty-eight, the same summer I met Liz. I had headed for Anemone Island on my own on a kind of self quest, and ended up incredibly lonely. I started frequenting the small Greek-Italian restaurant specializing in pizza and souvlaki because a waitress was friendly. That was Liz. She turned out to be my first client when she was accused of stealing from the cash register. If the truth be known, I had made up the story that I was a private detective, just so I could help her. Only later did I realize I was good at professional curiosity, and enjoyed righting what I saw as wrongs.

Liz and I met Faith later that summer, up in the hills one day when we were hiking. She was prospecting for gemstones and had risen up from behind some rocks like a kind of ancient mountain spirit, with the most leathery, wrinkled face I'd ever seen, a face normally resolved into a smile. She didn't smile often though that first summer. She was grieving for her partner, Almeda, and I think Liz and I provided her with some amusement and cheerfulness. Since then, she had provided us with the tower room as a hideaway, and her own brand of surrogate mothering. And this year she'd helped me stay sane.

I could hear the others downstairs, chatting away, even laughing, in Faith's art deco living room, clinking the beers, cognacs, and soft drinks which Faith would have immediately provided. I pulled the pillow over my head to block out the sounds. How could this horror have happened?

I loved Anemone Island, one of the jewels of the Pacific Northwest. It was large among the islands, twenty miles long and varying from ten to twenty wide. The regular residents were a close knit group of about four-thousand, mainly artists, unrepentant hippies, and retirees. In July and August, it was deluged with visitors—as many as ten thousand on a weekend. But the rest of the year, it provided good diving, gentle mountain walking, and solace for its residents and the few of us who visited. Of course, it suffered the usual pressures to build more tourist attractions and to log more trees, but Faith protected us from the politics when we visited.

Friday night, when we'd arrived, Faith had a wonderful poached salmon supper ready for Janeen and me. We'd decided we needed our comfort too much to stay at the campground with the others. We got our share of fresh air later that night as the three of us walked along the beach trying to locate constellations. I can never find more than the dippers and Orion's belt, but Faith patiently pointed out others, as she had so many times.

Yesterday, in the ocean, everything had begun to knit back together for me. The party Saturday night up at Jay's campsite had been fun too. Everybody brought whatever they wanted to eat and cooked it over a roaring wood fire on a giant grate that Faith provided. To encourage her students to enjoy a healthy party, Jay, as always, had brought a couple of coolers full of fruit juice and the five percent beer she referred to as *unleaded*. I've been on dive expeditions where there's been as much beer drinking as diving, but Jay ran a healthy and safe camp. I'd seen her warn a diver to lay off booze, and I'd also seen her refuse to let someone dive with a hangover. Not that she was a puritan. She was always happy to share a drink with her students, some of whom brought the most exotic liquor they could find to celebrate their dive certification. We'd shared some very peculiar concoctions over the years. Jay encouraged students to indulge in moderation and to have a good time. The stacks of good dancing CDs she played on her ghetto-blaster—everything from jive to Quebecois fiddle music—kept everybody dancing so vigorously that her campground parties were guaranteed to be successful and healthy.

Some people paired off, of course. I watched a little enviously as Danielle and Sally sat quietly, back from the fire, deeply engrossed in conversation. It was obvious that they were still a new couple, with all the deep staring into each other's eyes and the little body motions toward each other.

Tekla and Ginny were inseparable too. The senior Dales had watched from the sidelines in stony silence as Tekla taught Ginny dance steps to every song. They left, however, apparently too scandalized to watch, when Sally and Dani started dancing together. Then Dani asked me to join them, and we did a kind of sexy salute to the Dales' departure.

Even Jay seemed to be having fun, and that was a first. When I'd watched her before on these open water certification weekends, I had seen her intensity and even shyness, as she played her role as instructor, sitting back, a bit removed from the rest. But not tonight. To be honest, I felt ambivalent watching her.

Jay was as tall as me at five foot eleven, but slimmer, and she carried herself like the model she'd been as a teenager. Even after a day's diving, her shoulder-length honey-blonde hair was immaculate. Her brilliant blue eyes flashed from glamorous to mischievous in seconds. She always wore elegant silk shirts, like the deep royal blue one she wore tonight with beautifully tight blue jeans, and strode around her dive sites as if the whole world was her delighted, if slightly distant, audience. She was one of those always competent, always poised, always unattainable women that I found so attractive, alluring—so damn difficult.

I must admit I wished Jay didn't seem quite so happily heterosexual. She was flirting and dancing with Peter Demchuk, linking arms and tossing back drinks in mock serious toasts to every underwater life form known to humanity, and a few they were making up. "Here's to the purple spotted sculpin—here's to the bottle-nosed sea horse," someone said. I heard them laughing. I knew Peter was upset about Ginny's attention to Tekla, and I assumed Jay was doing her best to make his certification weekend a success despite that.

I didn't have much chance to talk with her. Once, I walked with Pete and her the fifty yards to the clump of trees where she'd parked the compressor, and watched as she put another pair of tanks on to fill with air for our Sunday dives. But she seemed so intent on giggling at Peter's stupid jokes, I felt embarrassed to be there and snuck back to my place by the fire. I didn't think she even noticed I'd left.

Still, it was a good party. As usual, Nazki took it as his

personal mission to entertain everyone. He told stories for a while; taught Sally, Dani, Janeen and me an Ethiopian line dance; then did some acrobatic dancing on his own that captured everyone's attention.

How could all that have changed to this? I couldn't think of any details that might have warned us that the fun would change to tragedy so suddenly. It was so like the nightmares that kept coming. I'd find myself in the middle of a deserted beach, endless white sand in either direction, endless turquoise sea and sky all around, making love with Liz. We would become more and more passionate. Then suddenly, it wouldn't be Liz but the huge wooden beams of a ship that I was embracing. The passion became a dreadful struggle to move the beams. Over and over I'd wrestle one up almost high enough to free her, then it would slip out of my grasp. I'd wake up drenched with sweat, absolutely sure I could hear Liz screaming.

Suddenly, I couldn't lie still any more, the terror was getting too close again. I got up and went to the window. Janeen and Faith were walking the others to their cars. I assumed most of them would take the ferry together, moving in a small herd for comfort. It didn't look like Janeen was leaving yet. I'd only met her two years before while masquerading as a janitor to gain access to some confidential files. She was a happy—though divorced and somewhat world-weary—heterosexual, but she supported my lifestyle, and we'd become great friends. She'd known more poverty and despair than I'd ever encountered, at least before Liz's death, and I'd come to rely on her earthy good humor and common sense. I could go downstairs now and have a drink. With just Faith and Janeen, that would be possible.

As I hit the bottom stair, I realized that Jay had slipped in while the others were leaving, and I would have run back to my room, but she saw me.

"He's dead. Tekla's dead," she cried out.

I dropped onto the couch beside her. "I know. We stopped

at the hospital."

"My god, I'm sorry, Cal. I wanted to help you to...to get back into diving. I never dreamed this would happen."

I leaned my head back, sinking into Faith's soft cushions, wishing I were anywhere else. But I could tell Jay needed to talk. "It's okay," I started and noted with satisfaction that my voice was steady. "You couldn't predict it. Where have you been all this time?"

"With the police. They wanted to know every detail of the whole damn weekend. What a grilling! Then I went back to the beach, walked for a long time, just trying to remember. I saw him, Cal, that bright green mask of his, just seconds before we roused the octopus. I was watching all of you," Jay's voice grew shrill. "I knew exactly where everyone was."

"I believe you, Jay. It's not your fault."

"It's my job to keep everybody safe."

"Can you think of anything you should have done that you didn't?" asked Janeen returning from sending the others on their way.

"No. That's what's so confusing. Everything was going great. Not like yesterday with Ginny's ear problems. Things were going well today."

"Try to relax," urged Janeen. "Nobody's blaming you."

"Corporal Hansen said I shouldn't leave town until after the autopsy tomorrow. He said he'd probably have more questions."

"That's only police procedure. They always want people to hang around for their convenience, right Cal?" said Janeen.

"Yeah," I sighed.

"But I need to be back at the shop. I've got customers coming tomorrow to rent gear. I don't want to disappoint anyone."

"I'll take the gear back," offered Janeen. "I have to be back by ten tonight anyway to do my shift with 'Top Drawer Janitorial Services'. Great jobs like mine don't come along every day, you know," she chuckled, trying to lighten the atmosphere. "Cal was going to drop me at the ferry, but I'll take your van and the compressor, and go to the shop in the morning. I can fill the tanks and rent out the gear for a day."

"And you'd better stay here at Faith's," I suggested. "You shouldn't be at that campground by yourself tonight."

"He can't be dead." Jay jumped up and looked around wildly as if she was going to bolt for the door. "I've got to go back to the hospital. They must have made a mistake. They must have."

Fortunately, Faith clattered back into the living room rolling her tea trolley loaded with a fat Brown Betty teapot, cups, and another bottle of her prized Remy Martin. "You've had a terrible day, young lady," she said to Jay. Her wrinkled face was even more creased than usual. "I'm going to give you a good stiff drink, then tuck you right into bed." Jay started to protest, but Faith waved her back onto the couch. "You don't know what you're about at the moment. I'm not having you up at some campground. Cal, you look like you need some cognac too. Almeda always said an ounce of cognac was worth a hundred doctors."

"I've got to get going," said Janeen. "Call me tomorrow at the shop if you need anything."

Janeen left and Faith gave us the large brandy snifters. Then she wrapped Jay in a gold and navy afghan. "You'll feel a world better in a few minutes."

"I knew where everyone was," Jay started again.

"There, there, dear," crooned Faith. "We understand."

"But it's not possible what happened. It can't be."

"What do you mean?" I asked.

"I saw him, Cal. It was silty back there, but I could pick out people's bubbles and masks...I swear I saw him, right with us. Then, when you found him, he was a long way in toward shore, he'd lost his mask and a glove, and he was dead. That must have taken at least five minutes, but I was checking more often than that. If it was really that long...it was my fault."

"Don't even think that way. I know how careful you are," I reassured her. "You know, there was something peculiar though."

"What?" asked Jay.

"When I saw him, the water was perfectly clear."

"Good thing too," said Faith, "or you'd still be out there searching."

"But if he was pulling his mask off in a panic, or trying to surface, or even if he had a heart attack, I would think he'd kick or struggle a bit," I pointed out. "And if he'd done that, there should have been a huge cloud of silt where he was. There was none, Jay, none at all."

"Unless I lost total track of time and he'd been lying there for ten minutes or more and the silt had settled." Jay slumped even deeper into the couch.

"I'm sure we only watched the octopus for a couple of minutes at the most," I said though I realized I hadn't checked my bottom timer through the whole octopus hunt.

"I need your help, Cal."

"What can I do?"

"I need you to find out what really happened. You are a detective, after all."

"You know I'm not that kind of detective. I spend my time reading files and unsnarling red tape for people. But I'll do anything I can. The autopsy will probably clear things up tomorrow."

"Cal, I have to know what happened. If I somehow let that boy die, I won't be able to live with myself."

* * *

It was eleven-thirty the next morning before anyone but Faith stirred in her jigsaw puzzle of a house, built by her life-long partner, Almeda Charles, in every architectural style she had admired from the 14th century onward. Almeda had been denied entry to architecture college in 1932 and spent the rest of her life designing and building bizarre houses at people's request, perhaps as a way of thumbing her nose at the male architectural establishment. Faith meantime had thrived as one of a handful of women prospectors in the coastal range, and the two women grew wealthier and happier by the year until Almeda died of lung cancer. Since then, Faith remained in their house, pottering about, feeding Aby, her large Abyssinian cat in his Gothic window bench, polishing gemstones now and then in the crystal palace room, and befriending younger women like Liz and me. At seventy-six, she could no longer head out prospecting for weeks at a time, but still made day trips into the hills, Aby at her side, both hiking with a reckless enthusiasm that left me dizzy.

This morning she was brewing herself a perfect cup of cappuccino in the post-modern black and red kitchen when I pattered down from the tower room. Jay followed.

"I've got the porridge on and the pot's already making more cappuccino," said Faith. "You'll want some cognac in your coffees now, won't you? A bit of an eye-opener."

"You certainly do trust your cognac, don't you?" Jay laughed.

"It's got you laughing," countered Faith.

"Yeah," said Jay. "Here's to a new day and plenty of cognac."

We sat down and Jay dug into the oatmeal. My head felt too heavy for chit chat or food, so I concentrated on letting the heavy crystals of demerara sugar sink into the white foam of my cappuccino. A sudden, heavy knocking on the back door broke the silence. Corporal Hansen and Constable Grove stood there looking uncomfortable as Faith opened the door.

"Why Eric, come on in," Faith said to Hansen, "and tell us what happened at the autopsy."

"Morning Ma'am," Hansen bobbed his head at Faith in a little boy gesture. I loved to see the way she intimidated men twice her size and half her age. "I've come here on the job. I can't stay." He turned to Jay. "Jennifer Campbell, I have a warrant for your arrest. You are being charged with criminal negligence, Criminal Code S. 220, in connection with the death of Tekla Takale. Come with me." It took only two steps for him to reach Jay. She jerked away, but just as quickly Hansen clicked a set of handcuffs around her wrists and pulled her to her feet.

"Now you just wait a minute, Erik," Faith said, loud enough to stop both policemen in their tracks. "You can't come into my house and drag off my guest without a word of explanation. I won't have it."

"She's under arrest, Faith. It's as simple as that," said Hansen. "A young man is dead, and the evidence suggests that her reckless disregard for his welfare was the cause."

"What happened at the autopsy?" I asked.

"You'll hear as soon as possible," replied Hansen.

"But Jay is never negligent."

"That'll be up to the court," said Hansen.

"Just how serious is this?" asked Faith.

"As serious as it comes. She could go to jail for life," growled Hansen, "but the truth is, the courts are so damn lenient, she probably won't even get two years."

"No," Jay tried again to pull away, but Hansen held her fast. "Calliope, please, help me."

"Take her out to the car and read her her rights," said Hansen, pushing her to Grove, then turned to me, with a mocking smile, "You'd better find your friend a lawyer. The judge will be in town tomorrow. We'll have a bail hearing then." He turned to go, then turned back respectfully to Faith. "My apologies, ma'am, for interrupting your day this way."

The kitchen was silent as we waited to hear the police cruiser pull away. Faith reached up and took my hand—I was pulling at my hair and hadn't noticed the pain till she stopped me.

"You do have to help her," Faith said.

I wondered if I could. For the last ten months I'd been

sunk in a fog, doing only the essentials for survival. But here was another death and another friend in danger. And this time, there was a chance I could actually do something to help.

Faith got up, took one of Almeda's impressionist seascapes off the wall, and began pulling hundred dollar bills out of its backing. Not trusting the banks since her family lost thousands in 'twenty-nine, Almeda had made a game of hiding hundred dollar bills around the house, particularly inside all her picture frames. Faith had taken a lot of the money after Almeda's death and bought term deposits and played the stock market. But she left some for emergencies and, she admitted, to amuse visitors. "Here's a thousand," she said, handing it to me. "That should be a start on getting a lawyer for that poor child."

"Thanks. From Hansen's tone, I better find someone good."

"Not on the island," warned Faith.

"I'll call Janeen. She'll know who to get." My legs felt hollow, my body like lead. "I...I guess I'm going to have to get into investigating mode."

"Right away."

"I feel like running upstairs and hiding under your quilt."

"But you won't, Calliope."

"No. I guess the first thing is to head down to the hospital to find out about the autopsy. Hansen sounded pretty sure of himself."

Chapter Four

I sucked in my breath deeply, to get a full load of oxygen, before heading into the hospital. I always feel uneasy in hospitals. I know it sounds primitive, but somehow I feel as if moving in this proximity to illness and pain is tempting the fates. Goddess preserve me, I thought, and punched the elevator down button. Morgues are always in basements. There must be some kind of architectural equation of death with the basement. Sure enough, the elevator deposited me across from a large sign pointing right to the morgue.

I pushed the door open, and there I was, for the second time in ten months, in a white and aluminum, antiseptic-smelling, icebox called a morgue. I leaned against the door-jamb fighting down my nausea. Get a grip girl, I told myself.

The wispy gray-haired man at the sink hadn't heard me over the rushing tap water, so I came in further.

"Hello," I said.

He jumped, then smiled. "Sorry, I'm always nervous down here. I'm too much of a believer in the supernatural to act as a coroner."

His voice was as wispy as his hair and as frazzled as his mind sounded.

"I always think the...um...spirits are watching me sort through their...well, you know," he continued. "Umm, are you here about the young Ethiopian?"

"I need the autopsy results. Was it drowning?"

"Almost always is under water."

"Something else then?"

"What's your interest? You're not the next of kin?"

"I'm a detective." I flashed him my license. "I'm investigating the death for a client."

"I'd rather you get your information from the police."

I sighed. Why couldn't people ever get it through their heads that most information was public. "I'm not trying to create any trouble here. Why not tell me instead of making me jump through hoops?"

"Corporal Hansen doesn't like people interfering when he's got a court case coming up."

"I don't mean to interfere," I said, trying a different approach, "but you may rub the skin off if you don't stop washing those hands."

The little man snatched his hands out from under the tap, then laughed. "I really do not like dead bodies. I know it's silly, but...."

"Why don't I take you over to the Swimming Scallop Inn and buy you a medicinal brandy," I asked, taking my lead from Faith's approach. "Then we can chat about the autopsy."

"Now that's a generous offer. My name's Binkley, by the way. Dr. Roger Binkley, GP, and medical jack-of-all-trades for Anemone Island.

"Cal Meredith. Let's go, Doctor."

Once seated next to the fireplace in the Swimming Scallop, savoring a double snifter of Remy Martin, Dr. Binkley relaxed.

"So, you suggest there was something else besides drowning involved in Tekla's death."

"I didn't expect to find anything else. Nothing in his general appearance suggested it. In fact, I wasn't looking very closely. I mean we do have drownings now and then. I sometimes wish the tourists would—"

"What did you find?" I interrupted. I couldn't tell if he

was enjoying building suspense or if he was simply unaware of my impatience.

"Once I got inside, sorry about the expression,...I began to notice some congestion and swelling around the brain, liver, and kidneys. I didn't think too much of it at first, but then I saw that his arterial blood seemed unnaturally bright, almost a cherry color."

"Carbon monoxide? That would be a shocker. Scuba tank air is the purest air available."

"Exactly. The last thing from my mind. Once I noticed it, I took some tissue for a look under the microscope. Sure enough, lots of microscopic hemorrhages. Normally, a person's skin and nail beds show up cherry red, so it's obvious. But with this young man, well his skin was such a deep black, no one would notice a flush. It would have been easy to miss altogether. I almost did."

"Good investigatory work."

He laughed, "It's only because I'm so damn nervous about making a mistake. You know, I hated pathology in med school. I just wanted to treat measles and broken arms. That's why I settled out here."

"And the concentration of monoxide in the blood?"

"Above twenty percent. More than enough to kill him."

"And whatever was in the tank would be tripled down at sixty feet under the water pressure."

"So I'm told."

"Then why would Hansen arrest Jay? The monoxide makes it sound like murder, or suicide I suppose, though Tekla never seemed that sort."

"Apparently not. Hansen told me the instructor filled all the tanks while having a drunken party. She must have got careless."

"So that's *his* theory." Suddenly, it made sense. Somehow Hansen had got drift of the party and decided Jay was an easy target if she'd been drinking. I remembered watching her with Peter. It had seemed unusual. I dropped fifteen dollars on the table for the waitress and stood up. "Thanks doctor. You've been lots of help. I hope you can take the rest of the day off."

"Just a pregnancy to check on. My favorite side of medicine."

I beat it outside and punched up the number of Jay's scuba shop on my cellular. I hate using those things in lounges and restaurants where people are trying to relax. I hoped Janeen would still be there, but the line rang ten times with no answer. I tried her home number, and she answered on the first ring.

"You've got to get back to the shop right away and call in any tanks you rented out today. Somehow Tekla's tank had carbon monoxide in it," I blurted.

"No tanks got rented. I had just finished refilling them this morning when the Victoria police showed up with a tele-warrant. They took all of Jay's tanks and the portable compressor. They went on a fishing expedition for files too, but didn't find any. I phoned Faith as soon as they left and she told me what happened. You'd already left for the hospital."

"Well," I relaxed a bit, "at least no one else is at risk."

"Except the store. I stayed and called most of the customers, then left a note on the door apologizing for being closed temporarily. But this is going to put one hell of a dent in Jay's business. Who knows when she'll get the equipment back?"

"I'm more worried about Jay herself. She was upset enough before, but this monoxide thing is worse. How the hell would monoxide get in his tank? Apparently Hansen thinks she was drunk. I have to admit, it all makes the criminal negligence charge seem less far-fetched."

"Have you talked to her?"

"I'm going to go over and see her now if I can. We have to get her a lawyer."

"My seventeen-year-old knows all the criminal lawyers in

town," Janeen said dryly. "He says Donald Feronne is the best in court, but that he's an obnoxious boor to his clients. He says Eva Nakolev has a one woman practice and is—I quote him—'a dynamite chick, very smart and sympathetic'. I've got a call in to both of them."

"You're incredible. Thanks. We need somebody good, but I'm not sure Jay can stand up to Feronne. I've heard about his courtside manners before. Use your own judgment, Jan, but get one of them up here for tomorrow morning."

* * *

I headed in a half jog—my fastest pace—across the road to the incongruous red brick building which housed the island administration, the library, and the police station. Up until five years before, all administration for the island came out from Victoria, by ferry. But the influx of tourists, especially to three new luxury resorts, required more attention than occasional visits could provide. So on an island renowned for its cedar and fir forests, some government engineer had built a red brick and concrete administration building and hospital, creating what he thought of as a village square. It made things neat and convenient for everyone, except for the old-time islanders like Faith who preferred all administrators as far away as possible.

The police office was empty and I punched the bell at the counter several times before a yawning Hansen struggled out of the inner office, buckling his belt. When he saw me, his face set angrily.

"Afternoon nap time, Corporal?" I joked.

"Maybe you slept, but I was up all night, tracking down details on this case," replied Hansen without a trace of a smile. "Getting warrants for those tanks for instance."

"For goodness sake, Corporal, we had no idea about the monoxide. Jay sure as hell wouldn't want to rent that tank to another diver. But she had customers coming today for equipment, so Janeen took them back with her to the shop. It seemed a reasonable thing to do."

"Removing evidence in a criminal investigation is never reasonable."

I caught myself just in time to stop tugging at my hair. "Look Hansen, I didn't know it was a criminal investigation. You know how I work. I'm not going to flout the law. If I'd had any idea those tanks were involved, I'd have been out checking them myself. What's eating you anyway? You're not usually so bad tempered."

"I don't usually have women like you getting people killed on my territory."

"I'm not real thrilled about Tekla's death myself, Hansen. And it's got nothing to do with 'women like me' if I catch your homophobic drift. As far as I know, Jay's perfectly heterosexual."

"None of you knows enough to stay in the kitchen. Young men don't drown in kitchens."

"Never mind," I sighed. This wasn't a discussion that would gain me anything. "I'm here to talk to Jay. She's my client."

"I'll have to search you."

"Get it over with."

I leaned against the counter and held my tongue as Hansen gave me a more thorough than necessary pat down. I knew he was hoping for some response so he could deny me entry. But I forced myself to submit limply and finally he led me through the inner office and down the stairs to the two cells at the back of the basement.

"Someone to see you, Campbell," he shouted, unlocked the cell door and pushed me in. "Holler when you're finished. Maybe I'll hear you."

I shivered. The cells were stark gray metal, about six by ten, with one small barred window onto the parking lot. The only other opening was a barred rectangle in the door, and Hansen had closed the cover on that. Besides that there were two steel bunks and a narrow passage way between.

Jay was curled up on one bunk, face to the wall. She didn't move. I knelt beside her and put one hand on her shoulder. With a shock, I realized I could feel a shiver tingle from the roots of my hair right down my legs. Since Liz died, Jay had been so generous with her time and her caring, we'd become good friends. We often went out to dinner or a show, or sat around Jay's condo listening to Bach, a mutual favorite. And Jay convinced me to come swimming with her three times a week and walking twice. She was a fanatic about fitness. But this was the first time I had actually touched more than her hand. I felt such a powerful attraction for this lovely woman my hand shook against her shoulder. I pulled away and forced myself to put on my most professional voice.

"Jay? Jennifer, are you awake? We need to talk." There was an indecipherable groan from the woman on the bunk. "Come on, kiddo. I know this is tough, but we've got to start sorting things out. Sit up and talk to me."

She pulled herself to a sitting position. Her face was waxy pale except for her eyes, red and swollen by now. "I killed him, Cal. It really was my fault." Her voice was a hoarse whisper.

"Take it easy. No one knows for sure what happened."

"Yes they do. The policeman said carbon monoxide poisoning. I must have done something wrong Saturday night when I was filling the tanks…got the intake too near the engine exhaust or something. I don't know, but…." Her whole body began to shake too hard for her to continue.

I sat down beside her and put an arm around her shoulders, straining myself to concentrate and comfort her. "Listen to me, Jay. There's no proof or even any clear idea about how the monoxide got into his tank."

"There's only one way. I did it. I filled the tanks."

"Have you told the police that?"

"I don't know. They've been asking questions ever since they brought me here. One comes in and asks, then the other comes and asks everything all over again. I don't know what

I've said to be honest."

"What have they been asking?'

"All about the dive, about Saturday's dives, about our training, about the party Saturday night. They wanted to know how much I drank at the party. The Corporal figures I was drunk when I was filling the tanks."

"Do you think you were?"

"I don't know...I know that sounds silly. I only had one vodka and orange. After that I told Peter to bring me straight orange juice...."

"So, don't worry about it."

"But I felt sick Sunday...almost like a hangover."

"Look, we'll sort things out. Just be patient."

Jay shrugged. "I can...face the truth. I'm going to have to." She started shaking again.

"Let's wait till we find out what the truth really is before you worry about facing it. In the meantime, I want you to listen very carefully."

Jay stared into the floor.

"I don't want you to say one more word to the police. A lawyer will be here for the court session tomorrow. Just say 'talk to my lawyer.' Nothing else, okay?"

"Don't waste money on a lawyer. It's obvious what happened."

"Jay, if you keep quiet until your lawyer gets here, we can probably beat this thing. But if you go on talking to the cops, especially when you're tired and upset, you could end up in jail."

"Jail! Damn it, Cal, I don't care about jail. Don't you understand? I think I've killed this boy who trusted me to teach him. That's worse than any jail."

I drew her close and hugged her silently for several minutes, biting back my own fears and desires. Then, feeling her body relax slightly, I got up. "I'm sure it wasn't your fault. And I'll keep working to find out how it really happened. Your job, in the meantime, is to keep quiet. Not a word to the cops, okay? I'll be back tomorrow with the lawyer."

"You're a good friend, Cal. I'll be okay. And thanks," she said, then curled back up, face to the wall, as I banged on the door and hollered for Hansen.

Chapter Five

Jay's court appearance the next morning was swift and relatively uneventful. Eva Nakolev had arrived on the 8:30 ferry. She was a tall no nonsense redhead, wearing a navy power suit, but carrying a soft, remarkably sensual, cream leather briefcase. She tried to talk with Jay beforehand, but Jay was barely coherent. Eva suspected Hansen had kept her up for questioning all night, causing sleep deprivation, but Jay wouldn't or couldn't confirm that. Eva pleaded her not guilty and argued convincingly that she be let out on her own recognizance. Unfortunately, the prosecutor argued more convincingly that the charge was serious enough to make a person consider fleeing. He made a big point that a conviction would cause Jay to lose her means of making a living and probably to serve time in prison—plenty of reason to flee. He pointed out that she had no family in Victoria. The judge agreed and set bail at ten thousand. Thank goodness Faith was ready to play guardian angel, or Jay would have been stuck in the Anemone Island lockup.

Then the judge called for an adjournment. Eva called me over, asked me in detail about the circumstances of Tekla's death, then turned to Jay. "I think you should elect to be tried by provincial judge."

"What?" Jay slurred as if she were drugged.

"You've got three choices: being tried by this provincial

judge here—the low man on the judicial totem pole, a superior court judge, or a judge and jury. From what I see now, I think we should take the bottom rung."

Jay just shrugged, so I jumped in for her with a quick question, "Why?"

"Several reasons. First, we go to trial much quicker; there are no preliminary hearings, just a straight trial. This will also mean there's a shorter time when her skill as an instructor will be open to question. Second, my technical arguments about the exact meaning of negligence will be understood by a provincial judge as well as by a superior judge better than by a jury. Third, if we go the lower court route, the sentence will likely be shorter if they do get a conviction."

"What do you think the chances are?" I pressed, especially in light of Jay's unsettling passivity.

"The police think they have a good case, but negligence isn't that easy to prove. I think Hansen may have been a bit overeager on this one."

"And what about the sentence if she gets convicted?"

"That's hard to guess. I don't know this judge. I'll have to ask around to see what terms he gives. But I'd guess less than two years, and I hope—hope, I emphasize—for probation alone since she has no prior convictions."

The court came back into session and Jay asked for 'trial by provincial judge' which proved she must have heard some of what Eva and I discussed. The judge then set trial for his next circuit of the islands and adjourned until then. I took Jay's arm and had to lead her out of the courtroom. She was moving like a sleepwalker.

Eva, on the other hand, charged ahead, calling to me, "You're going to have to get her to cooperate with me. From what I picked up this morning, the police think they have a pretty good case. I don't know much about diving so I'm going to need her to fill me in on a lot of key details, and quickly. I'll concentrate completely on this case, but...."

"She's still so shaken. I'm going to take her to my place

tonight. We'll call you tomorrow."

I loaded my gear and what was left of Jay's into my lilac Mini Cooper, the souped up classic car that Liz had surprised me with one spring morning when the lilacs were blooming. Jay, who had not spoken since we'd left the courtroom, climbed into the passenger seat and fell promptly asleep. I was just as glad. I really couldn't think of anything to say that would cheer her up.

It was evening before we reached my office above Market Square. It's doubled as my apartment since Liz died, though no one knows that except me. It's a funky old brick commercial building around a square where there are always musicians, sometimes theatre groups, and the best mystery book store in Canada. I suppose I should get a real apartment soon, but I tell people I work late. And I never let anybody beyond the outer room that serves as office, at least I never had until that night.

I woke Jay and led her through that outer room and into the living room/bedroom/den behind. I noticed my answering machine blinking furiously on the way through.

"Why don't you take a nice hot jacuzzi?" I suggested to Jay. "I'll bring you some of the cognac Faith sent with me. Then you'll be able to sleep again. I need to catch up on what's been happening here."

"I'm okay. The sleep on the way home helped. That old Mini of yours is amazingly comfortable. I thought I'd feel claustrophobic, it looks so tiny."

"She's still my pride and joy." I paused, then started carefully, "Do you feel good enough to talk about the weekend yet? We need to get working."

Jay took a deep breath. "Are you sure there is something to work on? The tank had carbon monoxide in it. I filled the tank. There is no other way for the monoxide to get in there."

"We can't just assume that, Jay! Could someone else have put carbon monoxide into it somehow? Or what about someone bringing an extra tank to the dive site? Couldn't that have happened?"

"You certainly are stretching your imagination on my behalf. I can see some evil villain hiding behind the rocks and dragging in a substitute tank just when Tekla went to pick his up. Thanks Cal, but I'm afraid the easiest solution is probably the right one. It's true enough—I wasn't really paying much attention to the compressor Saturday night. I've used it for so long I thought it was second nature. And…" her voice broke, "…and I guess maybe I did feel more drunk than usual. Maybe Pete made that first drink extra strong. I don't know. To be honest I think that lawyer wasted everybody's time with the not guilty plea."

"Did you fill Tekla's tank first or last?"

"I don't know. The tanks are all the same, you know that."

"But if you filled his tank first, why didn't everybody get monoxide in their tanks? Why only one? Tell me how the compressor works that you could get monoxide in one tank and in none of the others?"

"I don't know. For goodness sake, isn't it bad enough the police interrogate me around the clock? Are you going to do that too?"

I cursed my impatience for the zillionth time in my life and tried to explain. "I'm simply trying to show you that there are lots of questions yet. Just those few questions about the compressor could be enough. That's all you need, a reasonable doubt and they can't convict you."

"I don't care about being convicted. I just care about Tekla."

"I know. But we won't find out anything about him either unless you can answer some questions."

"Okay, but tomorrow. I'm too tired to think straight right now."

"Sorry. How about that jacuzzi?"

"Yes please. The cell smelled of vomit, and I can still smell it."

I got out a spare kimono, then showed her into the bathroom. This was my special hiding place, a magical funny oasis in the heart of the city. It was large, with steps up to the two-person jacuzzi that sat in front of a Gauguin-like wall mural of a jungle, full of tigers, parrots, and flamingos. I'd projected the mural on the wall with a slide projector, then painted it on with enamels and hardware store brushes. It had brilliant colors and the tigers fairly jumped out of the wall. The front of the jacuzzi was hidden by the few tropical plants that survived my tender care.

Jay whistled. "Wow. Do you hold orgies here?"

"Nope. I do my best thinking here. Do you think you can relax?"

Jay laughed. "Just me and the tigers? I'll give it a try."

While Jay bathed, I went to listen to the phone messages. Only one was about the case, and that was from Janeen about the police seizure of the tanks, old news. The others included a machine soliciting money for the SPCA—I might send them something if I got a paying job in the next week; another machine selling robotic kitchen utensils which I had no use for, not having a kitchen, only a fridge and a few essential appliances; and one call regarding a lost sibling case I hadn't quite finished. I promised myself I'd call that paying client in the morning and headed back into the bedroom, just as Jay emerged, flushed, from the bathroom. She looked fresh and scrubbed, and her blue eyes shone, emphasized by the blue kimono.

"Okay Ms Campbell," I said, ignoring all the thumping from my autonomic nervous system. "You're looking a little better now, but it's time for bed. In you go."

"I'll sleep on the floor," she said.

"Don't be silly. Get into that bed."

"It's yours. I can't put you out of your bed."

"It's a queen size bed, Jay. I may be a bit overweight, but there's room for us both, unless—" I stopped. My throat felt like it had been choked off suddenly. Jay had known about my relationship with Liz, and I'd always assumed she approved, or at least, understood. But we'd never talked about it. "Sorry, Jay," I started, hating myself for not realizing the possibility that she might believe any number of myths about lesbians. I found myself stammering incoherently and hating myself more, "I never even thought...I would never.... Look, I'll sleep out on the couch in the office. You're perfectly safe here—I promise." I bolted toward the office.

As I reached the door, I was stopped by a muffled sound that could have been a sob or a hysterical laugh. Jay was lying face down on the bed.

"Stay with me, Cal," she choked out.

I turned back. She looked so damn vulnerable, I wanted to hold her forever.

"I'm not afraid of you," Jay started. She sat up, grabbed my hand, and began, the words pouring out in a rush. "I...I know you've seen me dancing with the guys and flirting at parties. I do that because it's expected...easy I guess. But I've always known, I've just never said it out loud before.... I love women...I was always too scared to say. But then when I met you and Liz, I saw how happy you two were.... And Cal, I wished I'd met you first. I used to make up what I thought of as daring little fantasies about you and me. When Liz died.... I've felt so guilty about that, Cal. You can't imagine how guilty. I keep telling myself it had nothing to do with my fantasies, but still.... And since then, I've wished I had the nerve to say something...you know. Now here I am in your bed, not because you want me, but because you feel sorry for me. What a rotten joke."

I flopped down on the bed heavily and put my arms around her. "It's not a matter of feeling sorry for you. I'm just offering a helping hand, like any friend would," I said, deliberately avoiding the substance of her speech. I paused and took a deep breath, more to buy time than to calm myself. Nothing I could do was going to calm me at this minute. I knew getting emotionally involved with Jay was the last thing I should be doing. I needed my time and energy, not to mention some objectivity, to look at the evidence in the case. Besides, it seemed somehow unfaithful to Liz. But I couldn't slow the pelting beat of my heart. "However, this is not the time," I said carefully, "to be experimenting with your possible sexual orientation. You are too upset to think…'straight'. You said that yourself."

Jay pulled my hand to her cheek. "I've been imagining this for a long time. Please. You don't have to do anything you don't feel like. But please, stay with me, Cal."

I pulled off my clothes and slipped in beside her, pulling the quilt over us both. "Of course I'll stay. Turn over. I'll hold you."

Jay turned, and nestled her lean body, fragile as a lily-of-the-valley, into my ample one. I wrapped one arm around her shoulder, and stroked her hair with the other hand. My heart kept pounding like a jackhammer and I couldn't seem to get enough oxygen. Dear Liz, forgive me. I believed I could never feel this way again. I touched the firm swelling of Jay's breast, just brushed it with my fingertip. How smooth her skin was. My mouth was dry. I mustn't do anything more, I told myself. I mustn't take advantage of her. She just needs holding. This is not the time…As I struggled with myself, I heard Jay's ragged breathing become steady, slowing into a regular sleeping rhythm. Thank goodness, I thought, and turned away. Then suddenly, tears came in a cloudburst—for Jay, for Liz, for all of us—and I buried my face in the pillow to keep from waking her.

Chapter Six

The next morning, I jumped up at five, half an hour earlier than usual. Most days I try to do some waking meditations, a kind of eclectic combination of yoga postures, drumming, and goddess meditation directed partly at a little soapstone replica I'd carved of the Willendorf Venus. Not that I'm much of a mystic. I think I first was attracted by the thirty-thousand-year-old statue because her figure—all breasts, thighs, and stomach—reassured me about my own largess. Since then, I've found that spending morning time considering the good of Mother Earth centers me somehow for the day. That day I concentrated on a classic yogic headstand, hoping blood to the head would bring me more insight than I'd had the day before. Then I got a paper from the box on the street, and brewed up a cappuccino. As I debated whether to add the second sugar, Jay came in from the bedroom.

"How are you this morning?" I asked. "Would you like some orange juice? I squeeze it fresh."

"I'll get something on my way to work." Her tone was brusque.

I swallowed hard. I'd been afraid she'd respond like this. "Is there something wrong?"

"Nah. What could be wrong? Life's just perfect," she drawled sarcastically.

"Jay, I meant, is there some reason you don't want to stay for breakfast?"

"I've used up too much of your time already. I've got to go pick up the pieces at the shop."

I ran my razor-sharp paring knife through the orange, then stuck half on the old-fashioned glass juicer and squeezed. Jay's tone suggested she couldn't wait to get away from me. My heart sank. I was sure she was regretting her admission. I twisted the orange viciously and juice poured out. Thank goodness, I hadn't acted on her invitation...or maybe I should have; my restraint didn't seem to have made a positive impact.

"Look Jay, if it'll help, I can forget about last night entirely."

"I'll bet."

"Hey, I didn't do anything. I knew you were under stress. And I don't expect anything now."

"Let's just not talk about it—ever, okay?"

"Whatever you want." I popped two overdone slices of raisin toast from the recalcitrant toaster. "Have something to eat before you go. It's not going to be an easy day."

"Can't be worse than the last three," said Jay, but she took a piece of toast and began fiercely scraping off the charcoal crumbs. "I hate burnt toast."

"I'll make you another piece," I laughed.

"Don't bother," growled Jay, then started to laugh too. "Sorry Cal. Obviously I'm not in control. I don't normally make a fuss about burnt toast."

"The toast is a safe subject."

"Yeah."

I glanced again at the headline in the *Times-Colonist*, then back at Jay. "Why don't I come with you to the shop? I can help with what you need to do and find out some things about tanks and compressors while I'm there."

"No. I'll be fine."

"The story's hit the paper." I handed her the local news

section, then watched her face grow pale as she looked at it. 'Local Instructor Charged in Diver Death' read the two column headline over a picture of Jay being led into the Anemone Island courtroom.

She folded the paper without even reading it and placed it back on the table. "I'll be fine," she said again. "Besides, I have to deal with this thing. You can't baby-sit me. I might as well start today."

"Okay. But tell me about the compressor before you go. How would carbon monoxide get into the tank? How do you normally avoid it?"

"Do you really think someone could have sabotaged it?"

"I don't know—I need to know more about it to even guess."

"It's a portable compressor, built to be hauled around to dive sites. It's run by a gasoline engine and can fill two tanks at a time. It's ten years old so it takes about twenty minutes per set of two to fill them to three-thousand psi. But I've kept it in perfect condition. Sunday, I needed sixteen tanks for the dives and spares for...for emergency." She started shaking.

I almost reached to take her hand, then pulled back. "Go on."

"There's a hose, the air intake, that brings the fresh air into the mechanism...then a series of filters...there's even a catalyst that should convert any traces of monoxide into carbon dioxide, but it can only handle a little.... You have to set the air intake clearly away from the engine exhaust. I thought I'd done that. I ran the hose up one of the trees...but...I don't remember if I checked the wind direction. I always do check.... It took about five hours to fill all the tanks.... It doesn't matter, damn it. I killed him. That's all that matters."

"Stop blaming yourself and think for a minute. Did you have two tanks on the compressor all the time?"

"Sure. It takes long enough as it is."

"Then wouldn't the other tank be full of monoxide too?"

"I suppose."

"Then who had that one?"

"I don't know…. It must have been one of the spares."

"Do you know which tank Tekla had and which were spares?"

"No. They'd all been filled. It shouldn't have mattered which people took."

"Okay, we need to know whether there are traces of monoxide in two of your tanks. Because if there's monoxide in just one, it had to get in there another way, right?"

"True—but how…?"

"I'll see if I can find out anything from the police labs about the air in the tanks, and I think I'll have a chat with Peter Demchuk. As I recall, he spent all Saturday evening following you around. He could have seen something around the compressor that might tell us something. Will you come back here for supper?"

"No. I need to go home, act normally for a day or so."

"Phone me then."

"I don't need a keeper, Calliope. And I'm not going to waste your time. I'll be fine."

* * *

It took me an hour of file straightening and phoning before I'd tied up the loose ends of the lost sibling case and written the invoice for it. I needed some cash coming into the office as soon as possible, so I also wrote up some *Second Notice* invoices to slow-paying customers while I waited for a call back from Peter Demchuk at his co-op residence. When the phone rang, I was more than ready to question him, but it was Eva Nakolev on the line.

"I need to talk with Jay for a couple of hours," she said. "I've had a chat with the prosecutor for this case, and he thinks he has her cold."

"Did he say anything about the tanks?"

"As we expected, one tested positive for monoxide."

"Only one?"

"He didn't mention more. Why?"

"I think there should be two if it happened the way the police think," I told her. "I'll check with some other dive shops about their compressors and see if I can confirm this. What else do they have?"

"A signed statement from Jay admitting to drinking and not paying attention to the compressor."

"Shit."

"Exactly. And he says it's marked three p.m., though I'll bet it was three a.m. and Jay never noticed when she signed. I'm going to have to put her on the stand to cast doubt on that statement and that means throwing her to the Crown for cross-examination. She needs a lot of preparation."

"She's down at her shop, Eva. And she's really upset about Tekla."

"She'd better get upset about her own predicament or she can pack her jail clothes. I'll catch her there."

I'd barely hung up when Pete called and we arranged to meet at Maude Hunter's, a fake Elizabethan-style pub, a few blocks off the university campus. It was a long time since I'd been to Maude Hunter's, fifteen years since I was an undergraduate in the English Language and Literature Department getting an education I've used only for my own reading pleasure.

I slipped on a pair of charcoal wool pants, a soft rose and gray alpaca sweater, and a charcoal vest, before checking my appearance in the mirror. Not bad. I'd lost fifteen pounds in the three months I'd been swimming regularly with Jay and was beginning to feel fit again. I was pleased to realize I wouldn't look out of place at the university students' pub.

When I got there, Peter was arguing with a student about the need for international agreements against drift nets and for imprisonment of people who injured dolphins. I considered my new level of fitness and ordered a mineral water with lime, then impatiently followed it with a beer chaser while I waited for him to finish. Peter loved arguing.

"I can't be much help," he said when I asked him if he'd noticed anything peculiar about the compressor. "I wasn't paying any attention. Besides I don't have a clue how it should work."

"Damn. So, tell me how long you've known Tekla?"

"Since he arrived in Victoria last fall and moved into our co-op house. Of course, being a lofty doctoral student, he certainly didn't want to mix with mere undergraduates like me."

"Did he say that?"

"More or less. He always walked around the house as if he owned it and simply allowed us lesser mortals to stay there. One night at the pub, when I'd asked Ginny to go to a Dolphin Project meeting with me, he butted right in and said Ginny had better things to do with him. The guy had an ego like a hot air balloon. A woman would look at him, and up he'd go."

I tried not to laugh, but to take his young male bitterness seriously. It wasn't surprising. Tekla had stolen his girl. I wondered just how angry that had made him. "It must have really bothered you, seeing Ginny with Tekla?"

His face reddened. "She didn't know what she was doing."

"What do you mean?"

"He fed her all sorts of crazy lines about being Empress of Ethiopia. I can't believe she was so gullible."

"Empress? You mean, Tekla was asking her to go back to Ethiopia with him?" I asked, taken aback. "How bizarre!"

"He bloody well got her to marry him," Pete burst out.

"What are you talking about?"

He reddened even more till the tips of his ears were flaming. "Ginny told me about it at the hospital. I went to see her...before I caught the ferry."

"Did she say when they did this?" I was shocked by the news, wondering at the same time if this might not be the key to Tekla's death.

"I didn't ask. I know I'm not supposed to speak ill of the dead, but that bastard just wanted to get her into bed. Ginny was so pure and innocent. You know what, Cal, I'm glad he's dead. So there."

"You're pretty clear about that. Would you have tried to kill him if you'd known about the marriage earlier?"

Peter laughed. "You trying to find a fall guy to get your friend off?"

"I'm trying to find out what actually happened. And you're right, I don't believe this business about Jay being drunk and filling the tank with monoxide."

"She was drunk all right."

"What makes you say that?"

Peter squirmed, "Listen, I'm not proud of myself, but I figured she was my ticket into The Dolphin Project. I have to get a job there. The dolphins need me. She runs their diving program, but had made it very public that she didn't think they needed more divers, maybe not for years."

"So?"

"So I...I was playing up to her, a bit of romance, you know, to persuade her she needed me. I mean she is an older single woman."

"Thirty-one is hardly over the hill and desperate."

"Well, she fell for it. I kept pouring her triples all night. I didn't really fancy going to bed with a woman ten years my senior, but I figured I'd do it if that's what it took to get a job."

"What a lousy trick."

"I'll be the best scientist-diver they've ever had, Cal. I can communicate with dolphins. I just have to get that first job with The Dolphin Project."

My heart sank. Jay would have been very drunk. She normally drank very little. "Did she know you were pouring her triples?"

"She didn't ask. But she seemed to be enjoying herself," he grinned. "Acted like she thought I was Robert Redford."

It took an effort not to punch his Robert Redford grin. "I don't suppose it occurred to you that she might just be trying to help you have a good time on the weekend?"

"And I was helping her too—have a good time."

"So did you score, Mr. Redford?" I hated asking, but I couldn't stop myself. I knew Jay's sex life was none of my business, but I badly wanted to hear that Jay hadn't been taken in by this calculated attack. I also wanted to kick his arrogant head in. Too bad I'd dropped out of karate after the first three muscle-killing sessions.

"It doesn't matter much now, does it?"

"Someone may have died because of you pouring too much alcohol to get your romantic evening."

"Hey, I didn't make her drink. She's the one who harped on in class about not drinking too much on a dive trip. She could have followed her own advice."

"She thought she was. She thought you were bringing her orange juice," I growled.

Peter shrugged. "Give me a break. She had to know."

"What about on Sunday? What do you remember about the dive, Peter?" I asked to change the subject and get myself back under control before I did hit him.

"Jay was hungover, that's for sure. I caught her round the back of her van taking snorts of oxygen out of the respirator. She was embarrassed when she saw me. Then she admitted lots of instructors do that, to kick start their energy, she said."

"I didn't see anything wrong with her."

"I didn't say she looked sick. You want to defend her or hear what I saw?"

"Go ahead."

"Well, once the drills were over, we just headed off looking for the octopus. She would've swum right by it if I hadn't pointed it out. You know the rest. We fooled around with that octopus until Nazki turned up."

"Do you have any idea how long it was from the time you spotted the octopus until Nazki arrived?"

"No. But Jay was totally engrossed. She took her glove off so she wouldn't injure his delicate membranes. She was playing with him, hand to tentacles, even before you and Jan swam up. So it was quite a while."

"Wait a minute," I said. "Did Jay make a big point in class about the *gloves-off* approach when touching octopus?"

"She mentioned it."

"Do you think that could be why Tekla had his glove off?"

"That bastard wouldn't give a damn about injuring an animal of any sort."

"Come on, Pete, I know you didn't like the guy, but..."

"Who knows? He wasn't near us. He must have found his own octopus if that was what he was doing."

I didn't like any of the answers I was hearing from Peter. They all supported the police theory. And while he had a motive for disliking Tekla all right, nothing quite suggested a motive for killing him. I thanked him anyhow. "Give me a call if you remember any more details about the dive, okay?"

"Sure. And good luck. Your friend rid the world of a nuisance. It's too bad if she has to do time for it."

I headed out of the pub, then turned back on a whim. "Do you know if Ginny is back from the island yet?"

His blush spread again and he looked away from me for a moment, then seemed to decide I'd find out anyway. "She came back yesterday."

"Is she at home?"

Peter smiled. "She's in my room at the co-op. But she won't talk to anybody."

Chapter Seven

It took my full powers of eloquence to talk Peter into taking me to the co-op residence to talk to Ginny. As I drove, I wondered why on earth Ginny would go to Peter? She'd appeared to have no time for him on the weekend. And if she'd actually married Tekla.... But I guessed she wasn't thinking very well, and maybe any place seemed better than her parents.

More important for Jay, I wondered how much detail Peter had given the cops about the party? Probably all of it. I'd have to work on that assumption. I was beginning to dislike Peter intensely I thought as I pulled up at the co-op. It was a huge old building on Quadra Street that looked half house and half apartment. Years before, when government grants were easy to get, some bright student had organized a bunch of his friends to form a co-op and buy this building. They split it into twenty large rooms—some of them suites— and hired a manager. Since then, successive generations of students had become co-op members and lived out their university years in a secure, but non-campus locale. It was, perhaps, a hangover from the hippie era, but it also had the reputation of being well run and quiet, the place where studious types lived.

Peter signed me in and we headed to his room. Ginny was curled up in his bed, wearing one of Peter's baseball shirts that came down over her thighs, and half-wrapped in a quilt with dolphins leaping all over it.

"My grandma made me the quilt to take with me to college," Peter said shyly as he saw me take it in.

"Beautiful," I said sincerely. My grandmother had made quilts all her life, but she gave them away to every new baby born in her town. Maybe I had one when I was a baby too, but we moved so often when I was a kid, it had disappeared. I'd always been jealous of those kids who had grandma's quilts.

I pulled myself back from memory and looked at Ginny. Her curly blonde hair framed a face like a cherub's with what some would consider a cute pout. No wonder guys like Tekla and Peter chased her.

She stretched as we stood there and smiled without opening her eyes. "Peter?" she asked in a way that made me think she was transferring her affections rather quickly.

"Yeah, and Calliope too," grumbled Peter. "She wants to ask you questions about Tekla."

Ginny sat up abruptly, rearranging the quilt over her bare legs. I couldn't help wondering if her cute disheveled look hadn't been carefully arranged. "There's nothing I can tell you," she said. "He was perfectly healthy as far as I knew. And I didn't even go on the dive."

I sat down on the bed beside her. "I know it's difficult to talk about, but I really do need to ask you some things, especially about his background. Jay's in a lot of trouble."

"She deserves to be," snapped Ginny.

"Listen," interrupted Peter, "I can't bear to hear this stuff again. I'm going to play pool. Come and get me, Ginny, when you're done." He slammed the door as he left.

"Why do you say that about Jay?" I asked when Peter's footsteps had disappeared down the hall.

"Because she did nothing but flirt with Pete all weekend and ignored her students. And Tekla's dead because of it."

"That's nonsense."

"She just wasn't into it. She paid no attention to the problems I was having equalizing the pressure in my ears on Saturday. I could have burst an eardrum and she just said, 'Oh well, if you don't feel like diving, it's your decision.'"

I thought back to the Saturday dive when Ginny had the ear problems. Jay had actually spent a long time with Ginny, first trying to coax her into descending slowly so that her ears would be all right, then making sure she got into shore safely before taking the rest of us on the dive. She had even offered to take Ginny on a special dive all by herself and Ginny had refused.

"How can you say that? Jay did everything she could, short of aborting everybody's dive. And she didn't force you to dive and hurt your ears."

"You'd say that anyway. You're her friend."

Enough of this I thought. "Okay, I didn't come here to talk about Jay. I need to know about Tekla. You want to know what really happened to him, don't you?"

"No. It's too awful to think about."

"Ginny, Peter told me you married Tekla."

She started back for a moment, then reached under the pillow and pulled out a small leather pouch. "Tekla and I got married secretly," she whispered. "We didn't tell anybody because Mom and Dad are such bigots. But look," she opened the pouch, took out an intricately carved gold ring and slipped it on her finger. "The carvings are Ethiopian. It belonged to Tekla's grandmother. He said it would bring luck."

Thinking back, the marriage revelation didn't surprise me, given Ginny and Tekla's behavior together. I was more surprised that Ginny had been brave enough to risk her father's anger by going ahead with a marriage he would so obviously despise.

"When?"

"Four months ago. January 6, Twelfth Night."

"What made you decide to do that?"

"I loved him. And I knew Dad would never ever agree to

it, so it didn't matter if I got married sooner or later. Tekla said he was going to get a job at the UN after he graduated and we'd live in New York but travel all over the world."

"Peter said Tekla told you that you could be Empress of Ethiopia. Did you believe that?"

"I don't know. He seemed serious about it, but I didn't care. I just wanted to be with him."

"Where'd you get married?"

Ginny blushed. "Please don't tell anybody Cal, especially not my parents."

"What?"

"We went out for a special dinner first, champagne and stuff. And then we took the ferry and drove to this little town with an old white wood church. I think we drove for hours, but to be honest, I can't remember where we were. I don't have much sense of direction anyhow. I guess it would be on the marriage certificate. Tekla has…had it."

I couldn't stop my laugh. "You sure do a job of it when you throw over the traces, don't you? Do you think your father would be angrier that you were married or that you were drunk?"

"It's not funny. I've only been drunk once before. I tried to sneak into the house, but Dad was waiting up. He broke my nose that night."

Ginny was such an odd combination of rebel teenager and terrified preacher's kid, I wondered if she'd ever grow up to live a reasonably sane life. Especially with her father…

"Nice guy for a preacher," I said tentatively.

"He believes in punishing evil wherever he sees it."

"Is that why you came here, to Pete's?"

"I told Mom about Tekla and me. She said she'd tell Dad and then call me when it was safe to come home."

I could feel prickles up the back of my neck. Religion is a fine thing if it makes you more moral and kind and loving. But this taking on the role of the punisher of evil is frightening. Poor Ginny. Her first try at escaping with a husband hadn't worked out well at all.

"Was your father often violent?"

"He punishes us, Mom and me, if that's what you mean. But we deserve it," she added protectively. "One time he broke Mom's arm, but only because she'd lied to him about buying me new clothes."

I chose my words carefully, "Do you think he might have wanted to punish Tekla?"

"You mean would he have tried to kill him?"

"Yes."

"If he'd known about us...yes. But he didn't, did he? Jay took care of that for him."

"Are you certain he didn't know? Could he have followed you or found your ring in your room or something like that?"

"No. I'm sure."

"Okay. How about telling me what you know about Tekla's background. Who were his friends here? Did he have any enemies?"

"Besides my Dad?"

"Yes."

"None. He was such a sweet man, always polite, with that wonderful London accent he'd picked up. And always considerate. Why are you asking all this anyhow? It was just a horrible accident."

"I don't think it was an accident, Ginny."

"Why?"

"Because I've known Jay for five years, seen her teach, seen her dive, seen her take care of students. I simply cannot believe this happened the way the police are suggesting. And if it wasn't an accident, then it had to be murder. I don't think Tekla would have committed suicide."

"Of course not."

"I need to know everything you know about him. Were there people he kept in touch with in London or at home?"

"We never talked about that sort of thing. He always said

he didn't want me worrying about the hard life of his people. He would take care of that. So we just talked about us and our...." Ginny's voice cracked. "We talked about our future, Cal, and now it will never happen." Ginny rolled herself face down into the pillow and sobbed.

I forced myself to breathe deeply. How easily my grief was stirred again. I put a hand on Ginny's shoulder. I should be kinder to her I thought. "I'm sorry. I know some of what you're feeling and I know there's nothing I can say that will make those feelings any better. Come and talk to me any time you feel like it though. We can maybe help each other. And good luck, Ginny." I got up and was pulling on my jacket when Ginny spoke again.

"Nazki would know about Tekla's other friends. If it wasn't Jay, I want to know who killed him, Cal. I want whoever it was punished."

"I will talk to Nazki. Do you know where he stayed?"

"He shared a room here with Tekla."

* * *

As I started down the staircase, I could hear an argument echoing from the front hallway. It sounded like Nazki shouting the loudest, so I ran the rest of the way down. There was a group of about ten young men confronting the manager in his office by the front door.

"What's happened?" I asked the nearest young man.

"My room's been broken into," shouted Nazki, "and this creep didn't see any strangers come into the building."

I looked around at the angry faces of the other young men and decided this was no time to suggest the culprit might have come from within. "When were you in there last?"

"Last Friday," said Nazki. "I stayed on the island until today. I just wasn't ready to come back here."

"You must be very upset about Tekla."

"I needed time to think."

"Have you tried to contact his family?"

"I haven't had time," Nazki snapped, then relaxed a bit. "Sorry, I'm upset. My room is a shambles."

"You shared the room with Tekla?" I asked.

"That's the worst. His stuff is everywhere."

I began to feel the kind of tightening knot in my stomach that I always get when something in a case is important. "Can you show me the room, Naz? Someone may have been searching for something of Tekla's. This could have something to do with...with his death."

The whole group followed Nazki up the three flights of stairs to the large pent-attic that Tekla and Nazki had shared. I pushed ahead and stood in the door, barring their entry. Every drawer was on the floor, dumped out. Papers and shreds of paper were everywhere. All the clothes, bedcovers from the two beds and books from bookshelves were on the floor too. A large woven tapestry had been half torn off the wall. It looked like the perpetrator had been as interested in vandalism as in theft.

"You have to call the police, Naz," I told him. "This could be crucial. If someone wanted something of Tekla's, there may be a clue here. You'll have to go through everything with them to see if anything's been taken."

"I'll call 'em," said the manager, more self-assured now that the attention had moved away from him. "But they never do naught about problems here."

"They will this time," I said grimly. "I'll see to it." I turned to Nazki. "I need to talk to you. I need to know everything there is to know about Tekla. I'm more sure than ever after seeing this that someone murdered him. I need to know about him to figure out who would want him dead."

"There's about thirty million people I can think of," snarled Nazki, then laughed. "Of course, I shouldn't say that about the Emperor's favorite great-grandnephew, especially since we were friends. But there won't be tears shed in Ethiopia."

"Why?"

"It's a long sad story."

"Okay. Tell you what. I need to check my answering machine to see if anything else has happened on the case, but then we can talk while we wait for the police."

I headed back to the manager's office and dialed my office machine. Two more computers were soliciting donations and then I heard Jay's voice, shaking even more than I'd heard it already. "Cal, come to the shop, please. I need you." There was a loud click and the message was over.

As I started out of the office, the manager beckoned me. He was a man probably in his sixties, with a stubbly gray beard and matching stubbly hair. His accent when he spoke was undiluted northern England. "He did put a call in to Ethiopia, you know, m'um."

"Who did?"

"Young Nazki. I look after switchboard and all, m'um. So I…I heard 'im put through a call to Ethiopia before he come down 'ere shouting about his room."

"Do you know who he called?"

"The call hasn't gone through yet. Takes time in these 'ere foreign places. Besides I don't go listenin' to the boys' call, m'um," he paused, "but young Nazki calls there a lot and it's usually four, five hours before the call comes back for him. It's always to the same number. I thought you might be interested."

"Could you check if the one today was the same number?"

"I suppose. Though I shouldn't be givin' out the boys' information." His smile was a mix of pleasure at being part of some intrigue and hope that he might profit from it. I pulled out my card and a ten. He slipped them smoothly into his shirt pocket in one motion. "When time and charges come for the call I'll let you know."

"Thanks," I said, not really wanting to thank the sleazy old devil, but I was very interested in the fact that Naz had told me at least a partial lie. I wanted to talk to him more than ever now, and struggled for a few minutes trying to decide if I had time before I went to Jay's shop. But there was no way to tell how long it had been since she'd called. What had happened to cause the change from her independent tone of this morning?

I arranged with Naz to meet the next day for lunch and told him to make sure the police connected the break-in with Tekla's death, then sprinted for my car.

As soon as I reached the store, I could see part of the problem. Someone had spray-painted the word 'murderer' in ugly red letters across the window. The lights inside were all off. I knocked, then shouted. There was no response. I ran around to the back alley. Jay's van was there, but when I knocked and shouted at the back door, there was again no response. I pulled out my Visa card and started working at the lock, smiling grimly. At least the card is still useful for something even though I've gone way over my spending limit.

The lock slid back in seconds and the door opened. I kept advising Jay to get a deadbolt, but she preferred to rely on the alarm system inside instead of extra locks. I stared at the alarm box. No lights were showing. As usual, she hadn't turned it on. I headed into the store. Everything looked to be in place there, so I slipped up the narrow back stairs toward Jay's cubbyhole office.

A crack of light framed the bottom of the office door. I took a deep breath. What had happened? I swung the door open quickly, hyper-alert for any movement. There was none. Jay sat with her head down on the desk, her hand holding the phone off the hook.

"What's happened? Jay? Are you all right?"

She sat up slowly. I couldn't tell, at first, if she'd been sleeping, or was drugged, or in shock.

"They've suspended my license," she said. "I can't teach diving anymore."

"Until the trial?"

"Once I'm found guilty, they'll revoke it forever."

I'd known this would happen. I wondered why Jay seemed surprised. Perhaps just the reality setting in. Or maybe in the grief about Tekla, she'd never even thought of it.

"And the bank phoned," Jay continued. "They've canceled my line of credit and want it paid by Friday. And all the suppliers phoned. They want to be paid by Friday too—a couple offered to help me out by coming to take their stuff back."

I walked over and placed my hands lightly on Jay's shoulders. "Come on, kiddo. Come back to my house. I'll order in some pizza and tell you what I've found out today. I think there's a good chance that this was murder and that we can show that to a judge."

"I've worked for ten years, Cal, to build this shop. And now I'm going to lose it all."

I shook her gently. "Listen to me. There's a good chance that Tekla's death was not your fault. But you have to help us fight the case."

"Doesn't matter. I don't have the money to pay the bank. The business will be gone by Friday. I love diving and teaching more than anything in the world. It's the only thing I've ever been any good at."

"I'll phone Faith. She's amused herself playing financial wizard since Almeda died, and she knows all the bankers in the region. She'll know how to deal with the money end of things, at least till the trial is over."

"Sure, and then I can advertise cut rate prices to train with the killer instructor." Jay spoke in a monotone, like someone sinking deeper by the minute into an emotional coma. My anxiety burst out in anger.

"Damn it, Jay. You're saying no to every suggestion I'm making. I didn't think you were a quitter."

"I have no choice."

"Yes, you do. You can sit here and mope, or you can come home with me and start fighting this case."

"Well, I guess I know who to go to when I need sympathy."

"I don't do sympathy, Jay. But if you want help, you know where to find me." I turned and stomped down the stairs and out of the store. I hoped my exit might trigger some movement from her.

Chapter Eight

The first thing I did when I got home was call Faith and explain what had happened. As always, Faith understood instantly, and with her seventy-six-year old's wisdom, went straight to the heart of things.

"So you have to haul that woman—kicking and screaming if necessary—out of her depression before she makes things worse by just accepting whatever happens."

"Yeah," I agreed, mentally kicking myself, "and I think I just blew it by telling her off."

"Not necessarily. Being gentle and understanding may just encourage her grief. It is grief, you know Cal. Not self-pity. She's grieving for Tekla and for whatever image she had of herself as a competent dive instructor—which seems pretty important to her. And she's looking to you for support."

"It's just so self-defeating—this paralysis she's in."

"Remember how you felt when you were blaming yourself for not saving Liz?"

"That was different," I snapped, thinking Faith was pulling a pretty low blow.

"Not very," said Faith. "What pulled you out of your grief—that paralyzing kind?"

"I'm not sure I am out of it, Faith."

"You are."

"So what did pull me out?"

"Friends insisting you do things."

"You think I should go back to the shop and insist she come with me?"

"Better yet, pick her up bodily if you have to, take her to your lawyer woman and insist she talk. You were bringing her home to care for her. Insist she act instead."

"I'll see what I can do."

"Now, in the morning, get her on the phone to me. I need to know who her bankers and suppliers are if I'm going to convince them to hold off."

"Do you think you can?"

"Until the trial, certainly. They're just trying to get a jump on things, but they'll wait. After the trial...everything depends on the outcome."

I threw on my windbreaker and headed back to Jay's shop. It was still dark inside, but when I drove into the alley, the van was gone. Damn her, I thought, the tires of the Mini squealing as I pulled a U-turn. I drove carefully inside radar tolerance, a mere nine kilometers above the speed limit—which makes me a wildly speeding menace if you ask most of Victoria's retiree set—until I got to Jay's condo on Dallas Road. But the van was not in her parking stall, not on the street. I felt like throwing up. Where on earth had she gone? Surely she wouldn't have decided to run away, not when Faith put up bail for her. No, Jay wasn't like that. But she was awfully depressed. I could hardly think over the cacophony of mental curses my brain was throwing at me. How badly had she really felt? She wouldn't...surely she wouldn't have gone somewhere...not with the van, not with carbon monoxide.... I clenched my fists driving the nails right into my palms trying to fight back panic. Where would she go?

I got back in the Mini and started driving slowly along Dallas Road, looking to see if she was walking on the trail by the ocean. It seemed better than doing nothing. But there was no sign of her. I could see the Olympic Mountains rising up toward us from the States as they do on particularly crisp days and the sun setting in the ocean scattering pale yellow streaks across the April sky. Liz and I had gone diving with Jay so often in April, a cruel month above water perhaps, but such a brilliant clear time under water. Would Jay have gone to the ocean? Of course.

I squealed the Mini around again and headed to Henderson Point, Jay's favorite dive site. The entry is a rocky path, but the boulders and trees are picturesque, and a drop-off to eighty feet shows pink and green anemones and translucent giant nudibranchs, their white lacy lungs begging for photographers. It's an easy dive, sheltered from currents, and a good place to see the night life: ratfish, octopuses, and luminescent sea pens, looking like giant orange quill pens glowing in the sand. It was a guess, desperation maybe, but I pushed the Mini well above the speed limit this time, racing down the highway to the little gravel turn off to the cove. It was pitch dark by the time I got to the dead end above the entry. My heart lurched when I saw the van was there, but Jay wasn't.

I clambered down the path, picking my way carefully over the rocks in the light from the Mini. Jay's tarpaulin with her dive bag and clothes lay close to the shore.

"Jay," I started calling as loud as I could, knowing as I did how useless it was if Jay was under water. "Jay, come back," I kept calling, unable to stop myself. "Jay, come back."

The ocean was perfectly calm and the tide was low, so I could clamber a fair way toward the drop-off. The thick salty seaweed smell that I normally love seemed horrifying in the blackness. There were no stars visible and it was new moon. Wait a minute, I thought. If there are no stars, what's that light on the surface out there?

"Jay," I shouted again. My voice was louder, charged with hope. "Jay, is that you?" I focused on the faint light and began to believe I could see a dark shape beside it. That must be Jay. She must have gone for a night dive. "Jay, come back! Come back," I hollered.

Then I heard the first faint sound from the sea. It was a whistle. Jay's emergency whistle. Dear goddess, what had happened? The whistle went three times, then paused, and again.

I left on all my clothes but my shoes, knowing the cloth would provide some insulation without too much drag. I hoped I could trap some air, or at least warm the water between me and my windbreaker. The water would be freezing cold, but I had no choice. I glanced at Jay's dive bag—her pool fins and float were there. I grabbed them and splashed into the water, pulling the fins on as soon as I was waist deep. My feet cramped up almost instantly, but I fought through the pain, kicking as hard as I could. Thank goddess for my extra fat, I thought wryly, as I ploughed through the water. Breathe, stroke, breathe, stroke; I forced myself to focus only on the movement and the light.

The whistle sounded again. "I'm coming Jay. I'm coming. Drop your weight belt. Inflate your buoyancy compensator." Keep swimming, something told me. If I stop to shout, I'll never make it. Breathe, stroke, breathe, stroke.

Suddenly the light was right in front of me. How quickly I'd reached her...or was it quickly? I could see Jay thrashing, trying to tread water. "Jay," I shouted. "Drop your weight belt."

"Can't...taped it on."

I swam the final yards to the thrashing shape and shoved the float under her arms. That seemed to calm her a little. "Do you have your knife?"

"Yes."

I took a breath, then dived into the stinging salt, eyes open, grabbed Jay's leg and struggled to hold it long enough to find and retrieve her knife. I surfaced, gagging with swallowed ocean, took three deep breaths, and dived again. This time I grabbed the belt around Jay's waist. Numb as I was, I could barely feel anything, but I could make out a lumpiness where the duct tape wrapped around the buckle. I began sawing at it. Time stopped in the dark salt ocean. I felt nothing but bursts of fire through my fingers. I knew I had to cut all the tape. Was Liz under the tape? No, it was Jay, it was someone suffocating. I was suffocating, lack of air becoming a huge ball of pain in my chest. I kept sawing. Suddenly, the thirty pound belt fell away and we were floating. I could breathe. There was a light; I was swimming, but the light kept receding.

Then I felt rocks and barnacles against my legs; they tore my knees and I wanted to cry, but I was shaking too hard. Get to the car something said. Get to the car.

I looked down and saw Jay lying on the rocks. I bent over, loosened all the buckles, then pulled her up, out of her buoyancy compensator and tank, and across the rocks to the road. The Mini was there and its motor was going, its headlights shining out to the beach. Had I really left it running? I pushed Jay into the passenger seat, got in myself, and started to drive. My fingers were bleeding and wouldn't bend around the wheel. I must have cut them as well as the tape. It was so dark and I was so cold.

* * *

The smell was antiseptic so I knew without even opening my eyes that I was in the hospital. I hate the smell and the fear that goes with it, but the bed felt comfortable, warm and soft, and I was so tired. My shoulders ached. Why? Then the evening's terror flooded back.

"Jay," I called and tried to sit up.

"She's all right," said a voice from out of sight. Then Sally walked into view. She was wearing her hospital whites and stethoscope, looking very professional. I shivered. After surviving a childhood full of pneumonia and bronchitis, I still find doctors frightening even when I know them.

"You're both very lucky," Sally added, sounding stern.

"How'd we get here?"

"I don't know all of it, though I can guess some. You were

driving down the highway toward town, careening all over the road. A policeman pulled you over and found the two of you, both hypothermic. Jay was soaking wet inside her dry suit. And you were bleeding so much we had to cut you out of your clothes. He radioed for an ambulance and found Dani's phone number in your wallet. He called, so I met the ambulance at emerg."

"And Jay's all right?"

"We've warmed her up. She's conscious. I admitted her voluntarily into the psych unit. It looked like a suicide attempt, but I figured she didn't need any more trouble. This way, she can walk out when she wants. She won't talk to me."

"I've got to see her."

"You were near death last night. Stay put for another few hours."

"Sally, Jay was near emotional death and probably still is. I have to talk to her right away."

Sally pulled a vivid teal sweatsuit and thick 'farmer' socks out of a bag by the bed. "I had Dani bring these in for you. I figured you wouldn't wait."

I pulled myself out of the warm bed and worked my way into the thick fleece-lined sweats. My legs were cut raw by the barnacles and my left hand was swathed in bandages. Even getting into soft sweats wasn't easy. By the time I'd pulled on the socks, I was gasping for breath. "I guess that little swim did wear me down a bit," I joked.

"You should be in bed." She didn't crack a smile. I didn't know Sally well enough to tell if this was her normal bedside manner or if she was angry at me for some reason.

"Come on, where's Jay?"

"Fourth floor. Over in the Eric Martin Building."

"Great place for a psych ward. Hope the windows are locked," I said with a grim laugh. "Sorry, I can't stop my tongue from making these morbid jokes."

"The windows don't open at all," growled Sally.

We found Jay's room at the far end of the corridor and

found her bundled in blankets in a chair. A nurse sat across from her, playing solitaire. "I tried to interest her in a simple card game, but—"

"Cal," Jay pulled herself upright. "Oh Calliope, I'm so glad you're okay." She wrapped her arms around me and squeezed.

"That's more movement than I've seen all morning," said the nurse. "She's obviously not as depressed as we were told."

"We'll see her now. Thanks for watching her," said Sally, tactfully holding the door open until the nurse was gone. "All right," she said pulling up a chair and plunking herself in it. "I want to hear the whole story, right now."

"Look," started Jay. "I don't want—-"

"I don't care what you want," said Sally. "Right now, you're my patient, and I want to find out what happened. I'm damned if I'm going to let you do some fool suicide stunt that gets you and Cal killed."

Jay pulled the blankets tighter around her. "I've been acting pretty stupid, I guess. I.... Cal, hold my hand, please."

"Sure." I moved to sit by Jay's chair and took her hand in my good one.

"Last night, I felt like everything I ever wanted in life was lost," Jay began. "You can't imagine how that felt."

"Don't kid yourself," Sally snapped.

Jay shrugged. "The only thing that seemed still there for me was the ocean. At first, I just wanted to go for a dive...my last dive probably...at least for a long time. Henderson Point is one of the most beautiful dives in the world, especially at night. I've always felt totally safe there, in the water I mean. It's like the water protects me."

She paused and looked straight into my eyes. "I promise you, both of you, I didn't go out there to kill myself. But I did want to dive by myself—I've never done that before—just me and the ocean. It was when I realized I really couldn't get my drysuit zipper done up all the way across the back by myself that I started thinking how a drysuit full of water would sink a person. Then I put on my weights and…somehow I got the idea that I'd test the ocean. If it wanted to drown me, fine, that would be best. If I survived, then it would mean I should face whatever's coming. I taped the weights on so that I couldn't influence the decision of the fates. And in I went."

"How long were you in there, do you know?" I asked.

"I did a full dive. Three octopuses came and danced for me. There's so much bioluminescence from the sea pens at the bottom you can see quite clearly without your light on. It was so beautiful, I knew I didn't want to die. I wanted to fight back and find out what really happened. That's when I tried to surface and realized that my suit really was going to sink me. I had to fight all eighty feet to surface and then I couldn't keep myself there. I couldn't go back down because I'd used up my air. I guess I panicked, another first," she said bitterly. "I was struggling and sinking and struggling, and that's when I heard you calling me, Cal. You know the rest."

Sally walked over to the window and stared out. "You're a damned stupid woman. You nearly killed yourself and Calliope. All because of some dumb charge that any fool can see will get thrown out."

"What makes you think that, Sally?" I asked.

"It's obvious. Any of us can testify that Jay was very careful."

"I wish I was that sure," said Jay.

"Be sure. And damn well behave yourself, okay?" Sally demanded.

"I'll try…."

Sally bent over Jay's chair and stared down angrily. "You do more than try. You promise me no more of this nonsense, or I swear I'll have you committed and keep you in here until the trial."

"Okay, okay, " Jay whispered.

Sally sat down then and began to talk more quietly with Jay. It sounded like she was trying to get her to talk about her desperation, but I couldn't quite hear them, or maybe the effort was too great. At any rate the next thing I knew, I was back in my hospital bed and it was dark. I wanted out of this hospital.There was a lot of work to do if I was going to find out enough about Tekla to influence the trial, especially since I didn't have Sally's confidence. My shoulders and legs didn't seem to hurt so much anymore, so I tried to sit up. I was wrong. My whole body hurt now and I lay back down.

The next time I woke, the sun was streaming in the window.

Chapter Nine

I had to get going. For one thing, I wanted to catch up
with Nazki to find out what his cracks about Tekla's enemies
meant and who he'd phoned. It still took me much longer
than I'd hoped to pull on the sweats. I had to catch my breath
before I headed down to the nursing station to discharge
myself. I clearly wasn't as fit as I was giving myself credit for.
Still, I made it to the desk and must have looked all right.
Apparently Sally had said I could leave any time I felt well
enough, so they didn't try to lasso me back into bed. I went
to find Jay's room again.

She sat in the same chair, still huddled under the blankets,
though she too was dressed in sweats that must have come
from Dani, a pastel blue color that brought some life to her
eyes. The nurse was still playing solitaire, the same game as
far as I could tell.

"How're you feeling?" I asked.

"Okay."

"Good. Look, I'm leaving now. I've got some leads—"

"Take me with you!"

"Are you sure? You had a serious—"

"I need to help you find out."

"Okay!" I accepted, pleased with her change. Checking
with the nursing station, I found that Sally had arranged a
discharge for Jay too, having called Jay's emergency admit-

tance due to an accident not suicide, and twenty minutes later we were in a cab, heading for my office. Sally told me Dani had driven both the van and the Mini there.

I could barely contain my anxiety as I surreptitiously watched Jay. She sat rigid in the taxi, hardly even blinking.

"No more stunts, promise?" I asked as gently as I could once we were safely inside my place.

"I promise. I'm not normally so stupid," Jay said. She sat down on my bed while I looked for something to wear. I wanted to look sharp for the trip back to Nazki's, but I still felt cold.

"I've got a lot to thank you for," she went on, "and a lot of apologizing to do, Cal."

"Let's just forget the last few days and start again, getting this mess straightened out."

"Please listen. I can't just forget. I've got to...you know, straighten everything out, get everything in order before...before the trial. What's important is I want you to know that I...I'm really sorry about...." She hesitated, then took a deep breath and the words rattled out, "Oh hell, I'm sorry about the other night. I came on to you like I expected you to fall instantly in love with me just because I deigned to mention I was available. I'm not surprised you had nothing to do with the idea. I want to apologize for that and for being so offended when you didn't leap into my arms."

"You thought I was turning down your invitation?" I couldn't believe my ears.

"You did turn it down, Cal. That was very clear."

"But Jay, that was only because you were so upset. I was afraid you'd regret what you'd said. I felt like I'd be taking advantage of you." I sat down on the bed and put an arm around her shoulder, then figured I should try to be as honest as she was. "I guess...to be honest...I was scared too. I never thought I could feel anything for anybody again after Liz...and there I was, holding you, and feeling so aroused.... I didn't know what to do." I touched Jay's face with my good hand and began to kiss her. Her lips were soft and wet, and they opened eagerly. And then we were lying down, tongues exploring every contour of each other's mouth. I took her bottom lip between my teeth and nibbled gently, so gently, and heard her moan deep in her chest. Her hips lifted and rolled.

My heart was hammering against my ribs. I ached to press my hips against her, but...but I pulled back. "Are you sure, Jay? Absolutely sure?"

"Please yes. Undress me. Cal, see if you like me," she whispered.

I could hardly breathe with the pain of her fear. I took her sweatshirt and gently peeled it up, away from her skin, and over her head. Then I bent to kiss one dark nipple. I touched my tongue to the soft gathered skin and the nipple stiffened and grew. "You are beautiful," I whispered, drawing hearts on her skin with my fingernail. The answering ripples of her deep muscles beckoned me in. I slipped my hand inside her sweat pants. Her whole body convulsed.

"Please love me," Jay's voice was hoarse. "Please take me, Cal."

I could feel myself growing excited then, despite trying to maintain equilibrium. Somehow I felt I should stay cool, just please Jay, then quit. Somehow that would release me from the feeling that I was betraying Liz. I tensed my muscles, trying to hold myself still, then slid my fingers between Jay's legs and began folding back the soft wet lips, pressing in gently but firmly, deeper into her, until I found the hard pulsing center and began drumming; rhythmic, steady, quickening, until her whole body responded to my every touch. I could hear tiny yelps escaping as she breathed. I could no longer tell if I was aroused or angry. Why wasn't she Liz? I kept up the drumming relentlessly until I could feel that she was totally mine. Then I stopped.

"Oh god please," Jay gasped.

"Are you sure?" I whispered, holding back. I wanted her

to cry. I wanted her to feel the grief I felt even while I wanted to please her. I wanted her to know what this cost me.

"Yes. Don't stop, Cal. Please."

Starting ever so slowly and lightly again, hardly brushing her center with my fingers, I began drumming again. Second by second, I led her, harder and faster until she was crying out and beating her hips uncontrollably against me. Her frenzy lasted and lasted before she finally collapsed into the bed, gasping for breath.

I wanted to sit back, look at her dispassionately, explain how I felt. But the aching between my legs was too powerful now and my breathing too quick to speak. I slid off my sweats and pressed my own center against hers, spreading our lips with my fingers till they met, hot wetness against wetness. Jay took me in her arms, pulled me tight against her, then with one powerful movement of her legs, rolled me under her. I tried to escape, but she held me so firm, began her own drumming, stopped, began again, stopped, began, again and again, until overwhelmed, I exploded, hot and wet, and weeping uncontrollably.

"My god, did I hurt you?"

"No," I choked." I…. It felt…you were wonderful."

"But you're sobbing,"

"It's okay. I…I'm sorry…Liz…."

"Oh Cal, I'm sorry. I shouldn't have—"

"Sssh," I whispered. I began to realize the wonder of what had just happened and I could feel myself steadying. "Jay, darling, I've never felt quite like this before. It'll just take me a bit of time to…you know, get used to everything."

She rolled away and I felt instantly vulnerable. " Come back. Don't move away, please." I burst out.

"Are you sure? I feel like I've done something terrible to you."

"Something wonderful. Please Jay, just bear with me and know that my grief for Liz isn't going to interfere with my love for you…not anymore." I sat up to pull the eiderdown over Jay's naked body but stopped when I saw her bruises. "Your back's black and blue."

"The tank. I didn't tighten it enough so it was banging against me the whole time. Stupid."

"You must be in pain, Jay. I must have hurt you terribly just now. Why didn't you tell me?"

"No pain. Just glorious feelings I've never even imagined."

I wrapped myself around her, my breasts pressed into her back, and we lay silently together, breathing in unison.

It was two-thirty p.m. before I woke up. Jay was sitting cross-legged on the bed, staring down at me.

"You're tired," she said.

"I've had a bit of exercise."

"Stay there, please. I'll make you something to eat and then just sit with you while you rest. You're still exhausted from that swim."

"And you're not?"

"You did the hard work."

"I've got to find Nazki. I stood him up for lunch yesterday."

Jay handed me the phone from the bedside table. "Talk to him by phone. You don't have to move."

"Doesn't work. I have to see the witness's face as he talks. And he's not being completely honest. He knows something." I took the phone though, realizing suddenly that I was deep in a new relationship, almost without forethought, and a relationship with someone who was incredibly sensuous, powerful, and every inch my equal. Liz had followed my lead in things, and I wondered briefly how I'd cope with this new equality, then decided thinking about it now wouldn't help. I put through the call to Nazki, explained and apologized for missing lunch, and arranged to meet him at seven at Maude Hunter's.

"I'll set the alarm for six," Jay said, "and you sleep. I'll watch over you till then." She pushed me down and curled herself around me under the eiderdown. I didn't resist.

* * *

The pub was almost empty when we arrived and Nazki had picked a booth in the far back corner. He looked surprised when he saw Jay.

"I thought you'd still be on the island," he said.

Jay pulled a tight smile, "I'm out on bail."

"Good luck," Nazki smiled back. "I'm sorry you're being blamed. I agree with Cal. He probably was murdered."

"Did you find out if anything was missing from your room?" I asked.

"None of my things. I can't really tell about his. He had so much stuff filed here and there."

"Tell me about him." I went on. "You said the other day that lots of Ethiopians don't like him."

"You have to know Ethiopia and Tekla to understand that. My country...it's a very poor country and we have hundreds of different ethnic groups. We have Christians and Moslems and Jews and pagans. And they all fight each other, or at least distrust each other, always have."

"I thought Ethiopia was quite a strong country with a big influence in the rest of Africa?"

"Awesome under the Emperor, good old Haile Selassie, because he ruled with an iron fist, and an iron military. Did you know that Selassie's given name was Ras Tafari?"

"No. Is that...?"

"Yes indeed. The whole Rastafarian movement started back in the '30s. They figured Selassie was a kind of black messiah who was going to become Emperor of the world and raise all us blacks up to power."

"He must have been quite the guy. Did he encourage that?"

"How would I know? But he certainly acted as though he thought his will was the will of God." Naz laughed, "That was until his own bodyguard turned on him in '74. I guess you can't oppress people forever. Of course, the military haven't got his charisma and haven't been strong enough themselves to hold things together since."

"What's all this got to do with Tekla?" Jay asked.

"His great-grandfather was Selassie's brother."

"I'd heard that," she said. "So what does that mean?"

"He was seven when Haile Selassie was deposed and their whole family decimated. His parents were imprisoned, then killed. A friend of his mother's family raised him, and he used that woman's name to work as a minor bureaucrat in various government departments until he got the money to get to London and university. He thinks...thought...it would be his destiny to go back to Ethiopia after his Ph.D. and become Emperor. Maybe the new Ras Tafari, Emperor of the world."

"You're kidding," I laughed.

"Not at all. He had a few delusions, did my pal Tekla."

"But he never seemed even interested in Ethiopia when he talked," said Jay. "You were the one who used to tell us about the famine and the communist military and all that."

"He hid his ambitions well. If they'd been widely known, he would have been assassinated long ago. He was bright, ruthless, and careful...until that dive."

"Come on," I said. "Tekla was just a big playboy who spent all his time romancing Ginny. About as ruthless as a teddy bear. Who is this other character you're telling us about?"

Nazki hailed the waitress for another round and lit up one of the Gauloises he smoked. "You never saw inside him. Maybe I shouldn't say this now that he's dead, but you can't think of him as an ordinary Ethiopian, another guy just like me. His family, the Solomonic dynasty, was one of the richest and most brutal ruling families in the world. Made the Shah of Iran look like Santa Claus."

"But if Haile Selassie was so revered?"

"By people outside the country. Inside no one dared say

different. Listen, this was a family that had ruled since the thirteenth century. And they trace their ancestors back to when King Solomon tricked and raped the Queen of Sheba. They're proud of that. It's their dynastic founding story, can you believe it? And some sycophantic hangers-on think they should be restored to power. So just because he was a member of that family, Tekla would have had a good chance to take over if he'd played his cards right. And he intended to do just that."

"But Ginny said he planned to get a job with the UN and live in New York." I could hardly imagine the modern soft-spoken Tekla that I knew being part of a seven hundred year old dynasty, let alone ambitious or ruthless.

"Ginny is an idiot. He was just playing with her so he didn't have to…well, you know, he always had women—"

"But he married her," I broke in.

"What?" Nazki laughed.

"It's true. I saw her ring, his grandmother's," I said.

"If he did, it was only a convenience as far as I can see," laughed Nazki. "Tekla cared about only one thing in the world, being Emperor, and he would do anything to get there."

"You don't sound like you liked him very much, Naz," I asked. He was certainly being candid about Tekla—if he was telling the truth.

"You wanted the truth from me, right?" he said, mind reading, "not some sort of maudlin sentiment? Besides when you're a foreign student, you like anybody who comes from your country. You need each other's support."

"Did you plan to be part of his entourage when he became Emperor?"

"An ambassador, maybe. But I can get there on my own."

I took a gulp of beer and sat silently for a few minutes. Nazki's story was a total surprise. He and Tekla had always appeared to be best of friends when the dive class had parties. Now he was talking as if he merely tolerated him. I wondered suddenly if he was frightened.

"If you think Tekla was murdered because of his ambitions," I asked, "do you think you're in danger now because you were associated with him? Are you frightened, Naz?"

"Nope, I'm not even from the same people. He was Amhara. I'm Beni Amer. A Beni Amer wouldn't be Emperor."

"I guess I wonder, then, if you thought he was so ruthless and all, why you were friends?"

Nazki smiled, but it was a cold smile. "I needed a rich friend and he had millions in Swiss banks. He needed friends of any sort. He was very lonely in his self-deluded world."

I gulped, "Sorry. I guess I'm looking for something solid to go on. What you've given me is a very different picture of Tekla than I got from Ginny and it does explain why he'd have enemies, I guess. But it doesn't help me explain what happened Sunday. How would some political rival get carbon monoxide in Tekla's tank?"

"That's for you to find out, isn't it?"

Suddenly, Nazki's cold assessment of his *friend* frightened me. Apparently neither he nor Tekla were the straightforward, nice young men I'd assumed. I wanted to get away so I could assess this new information. "Just one more question, Naz. The other day at the co-op, you told me you hadn't had time to contact Tekla's family, but I understand you did have time to phone Ethiopia. Who were you calling?"

"My mother. I'm a very devoted son. And Tekla has no family to speak of or I would have called them. The embassy was notified, of course, but by the Canadian authorities, not by me."

So much for that idea, I thought. "I guess we've taken enough of your time," I said. "If you have any other thoughts about this, let me know. Come on Jay. I'm ready for home."

We got up and were heading for the pub door when we heard Nazki call in his familiar laughing voice, "Of course, if you want to talk to someone who had good reason to kill him, talk to the lady doctor."

I whirled around and was back at the table in three steps. "Do you mean Sally? What would she have to do with him?"

Nazki smiled. "She worked with him in Ethiopia. And then left the country very suddenly. If I was looking for a suspect, I'd talk to her."

Chapter Ten

"Sally sure kept her connection with Tekla a very deep secret. This may be the break we've been hoping for." I spoke calmly as we reached my apartment, but inside I was both furious and excited that she hadn't mentioned her Ethiopian connection. It had to be important. I walked straight to my phone and dialed Dani's number.

"I have to talk to Sally right away," I said when Dani answered.

"She left at noon to give some lectures up the coast on using nurse practitioners in remote areas. She won't be back until tomorrow. Why don't you come over for dinner then?"

It felt bad suddenly, suspecting my friend's lover. I tried to keep my voice even. "It's not really a social chat I'm looking for."

"That's all right. We can spend five minutes on business."

I grimaced. I'd begun to like Sally—she'd been super at the hospital. But I wanted to get her away from Dani so I could put the heat on her, and there wasn't much time. "Dani," I couldn't help apologizing. "I'm sorry, but I need to talk to her alone."

"We have no secrets, Cal."

"She knew Tekla long before the dive class. I need to ask her some questions."

"No she didn't. She would have told me." Dani's voice

sharpened. "Don't go hunting for suspects here."

"I just need to ask some questions. I'll be as brief and gentle as I can, Dani."

"Oh shit. I told her she should have told the cops about the counseling. But she insisted it was strictly doctor-patient stuff, completely privileged."

"Counseling? Yeah right," I said, hoping to sound confident enough that Dani would explain.

"Counseling Tekla. Isn't that what you wanted to ask her about?"

"Yeah. That...and a few other things." Plenty of other things, I thought. Clearly Sally had had a lot more to do with Tekla than she'd let anyone know.

"Well, come on over about five. And listen, you're the best friend I've ever had, Cal, but don't try harassing my lover. I won't have it."

* * *

Saturday was lost as far as I was concerned. I still felt too tired and sore to do anything energetic and only managed fifteen minutes of yoga stretches in the mornings. I never really function properly when I don't follow through my morning routine, but I gave up meditating after five frustrating minutes of chasing my brain stylus through a zillion wrinkles of gray matter. So much for stilling the mind.

I went with Jay to the dive shop and started inventory. Faith had convinced the bankers to stand pat, but suggested we inventory as much as possible ahead of time, just in case the trial went badly and Jay decided she had to sell the shop. Counting regulator mouthpieces was not my idea of an exciting time and Jay didn't appear to have any records to check our numbers against anyway. Apparently, she kept the whole inventory in her head. That would impress the bankers, I thought. Even more frustrating was the fact that this stock counting wasn't helping figure out what happened to Tekla, especially since we couldn't inventory the tanks which were still with the cops.

With so little still to go on, I ached with impatience at what Sally might tell us. By five o'clock when we drove up to Dani's house, I was ready to jump on anybody who offered a lead—and fighting PMS as well.

Sally greeted us at the door with a platter of smoked oysters and baby clams all toothpick-skewered onto rye bread. "Hi you two. You're looking better. How are you feeling, Jay?

"I'm okay," Jay smiled. "Thanks."

"With luck, you'll be even better after the trial." Sally added.

"I need to talk to you privately, Sally," I said abruptly, dispensing with the small talk. " Let's do it now and get it over with."

"Let's not," Sally whirled away and hit the play button on the CD. The hot piano of Oscar Peterson belted out of the speakers. "I've worked like a dog for days. I can't bear to do anything serious again until at least next week."

I couldn't tell if she'd been warned by Dani that I had questions or if she was really just burned out. "This can't wait," I said evenly.

"Anything can wait—except babies. Any doctor knows that in this age of cutbacks," Sally laughed. "Come on into the kitchen and I'll get you drinks. We've got everything."

The dam broke. My irritation cascaded out. "Okay Sally, if you don't want to talk in private, we'll talk in public. What happened between you and Tekla when you worked with him in Ethiopia?"

Sally's face turned white and she dropped into the nearest chair. Obviously, Dani hadn't warned her.

"Ethiopia?" repeated Dani as she swung out through the kitchen door carrying a crystal bowl of chips and dip. "You were never there, were you?"

"Yes she was," I said.

Dani quickly sat down on the arm of the chair and patted Sally's shoulder, growling, "Don't push, Cal."

"I told you I had to ask some questions. I still have to."

"How did you find out?" Sally whispered.

"Nazki told me."

"I didn't think he knew."

"He said you left the country in a hurry. Was Tekla black-mailing you about something?" I asked. "Is that what happened?"

"Not really. Not exactly. I...." She paused and I waited, knowing silence was my best ally here. "It's all so awful...."

Dani took Sally's hand and held it between her own. "Tell us. No matter how bad it is, Sal, I'll support you. I've told you that before."

Sally shivered as if caught in a sudden wind and said nothing. I felt like a first rate bitch.

"If this has no bearing on Tekla's death, it'll stay between us," I promised.

"Oh god, Dani, I never wanted you to hear about this."

"Come on, Sally," I encouraged.

"I had just finished my internship," she started finally, "and I had a chance to do a six month locum with Medic-Aid in Ethiopia. I jumped at it. Tekla was the Ethiopian in charge of the health department in the province where I was—Tigre, south of Eritrea. Just a young guy with good connections, I thought. We...we spent a lot of time together. I guess you could say we dated, though it wasn't really like that, at least I didn't think so. I was just trying to get him to bring in more equipment and medicine, and he was always telling me why he couldn't." Sally paused and took a deep breath.

"Go on," Dani urged.

"He came to my quarters one night and...and to put it simply, he raped me. He made it clear that no mere woman was going to turn down a future ruler of the country." She turned her face away from all of us, but I could see the muscles bunched around her jaw. "Apparently, he thought I'd led him on."

"My poor darling, no wonder you never talked about

this." Dani wrapped her arms around Sally's shoulders.

"What happened then?" I pushed.

"For god's sake, Calliope!" Dani said.

"I better tell the whole story now…. I couldn't sleep after he left. I thought about killing myself. I was so humiliated I couldn't bear the thought of facing him again. But…but I try to be a survivor. I decided to tell the local army commander and ask for protection. How bloody naive. Two days later, the police arrested me for diverting drugs in return for bribes. They searched my quarters and planted thirteen thousand dollars in marked bills from a sting operation they said they'd been doing and two boxes of drugs that had gone missing." Sally turned back and looked straight at me as she continued. "I was lucky I guess. They didn't bother with a trial. They took me straight to Addis Ababa and put me on a plane to France. There were a few reports in the Ethiopian and French newspapers about a dishonest doctor being deported, but nothing else. I stayed in France for a while. I was so stunned at first I didn't know what to do. Then I realized I was pregnant. So I went to Holland long enough to have an abortion and recover. And then I came home, moved out here to the coast where nobody knew me, and set up my practice. That's the story."

I felt sick to my stomach, and Oscar Peterson banging away on the ivories wasn't helping. I went over and punched the stop button. I knew I had to push on. This was a perfect motive for murder. "So the only public records about any of this say you were thrown out for accepting bribes?"

"Of course. That was the public version."

"Why on earth were you counseling him?" Dani asked.

I was sure Sally shot Dani a dirty look in reply, but maybe it was a response to the whole situation. She slumped further down into her chair.

"It seems like an odd thing to do, given the circumstances." I added.

"He came to me and asked to talk. I think because I was

the only doctor he knew here. Professionally, I couldn't refuse. He was terribly upset."

"So, what was it about?"

"That's doctor-patient material. It's confidential."

"This could be a murder or a suicide. That—"

"Doesn't matter. I can't betray my patient's confidence."

"Bullshit," I exploded.

"It must have been horrid for you when you first saw Tekla again," Dani interrupted.

"It was one of the worst moments of my life, seeing him standing there by the pool on the first night of the dive class. I begged you to quit, remember?"

"Yeah, you told me you were claustrophobic," added Dani, "deathly afraid of getting into the gear until Jay found you that wrap-around see-through mask."

"That's right. You looked awful that night. I actually didn't think you'd come back," said Jay.

Dani ran her fingers through Sally's hair. "I'm sorry, love. I thought it was something you could deal with."

"Never mind. It really didn't matter," sighed Sally.

"I'm sure Tekla recognized you that first night," I persisted.

"He came over during coffee break. He looked me straight in the eye and said 'I can still ruin your career any time I want. So remember to do what I ask.'"

"That bastard," Dani burst out. "You should have told me."

"I couldn't bear to talk about it."

"And besides," I carried on, "there's no record of any rape, just of bribes and drug diversions, right?"

"Calliope, give it a rest," Dani snarled.

"Never mind. She's right." Sally stared at the floor. "He could easily have gone to the Medical Association—and they would have tossed me out on my ear, or at least suspended me for so long it would be the equivalent. And besides, I'd just gotten to know you, Dani. I didn't know if you'd believe his version or mine. I was afraid you'd believe him."

"Never. My poor love, no wonder you have trouble trusting people."

"And so you killed him." I interrupted, wishing Dani would punch me out, wishing I didn't have to do this.

"No." Sally's voice dropped to a whisper. "I'm a doctor. I don't...kill people. I...I'm glad he's dead. I even wished I could kill him. But I didn't."

"Come on, Sally, don't joke with me. You had all the motive in the world. More than most. Some people would even think you were justified...if the rape story is true," I said, trying not to hear myself.

"I knew you wouldn't believe it."

Danielle stood up abruptly. "You have to go now Cal. I'm not listening to that."

"What about Jay? Will you just let her go to jail for this?"

"They'll never make that negligence charge stick. I've seen them try it on doctors. It's just to make them look good when they've got no one else to arrest," Sally muttered.

"I'm trying to get to the bottom of a crime, the killing of a young man. And you, Sally, had a very strong motive to want him dead."

"And no opportunity to do anything," Dani intervened. "We weren't near the tanks and neither of us knows a damn thing about compressors. Forget it, Cal. I wish you luck, but not on Sally's back. Now get out of here. I don't want to talk to you for a while."

With that we headed back to the car, dinner forgotten

"You came on a bit strong, don't you think?" Jay asked once we were driving.

"Strong?" I exploded. "You're trial is coming up very fast and so far I have nothing to suggest as an alternative cause of death. I would've come on a lot stronger if I'd had anything more to push her with."

"I still don't like it. We don't need to browbeat others to get me off, do we?"

I felt like throwing up—obviously hormones. It couldn't all be guilt at haranguing Sally. "You're such a gentle soul, Jay, and probably right. I guess I did come on too strong. Goodness knows the poor woman had a tough go of it, whatever happened in Ethiopia. But what on earth would she be counseling him about? That's bizarre."

Jay was silent for the rest of the drive. Probably digesting the experience of seeing me at my suspicious worst. We'd agreed to go to her condo for the night, and once we got there, she went straight to get ready for bed. I brought Faith's cognac bottle into the bedroom.

"Do you want a snifter before you sleep?"

"Sure," Jay was standing at the window staring out to the Juan de Fuca Strait. She was silent for a long time and I felt I shouldn't interrupt her. Finally, after about five minutes, she sighed and turned back to me. "Cal, what about Ralph Dale, Ginny's father?"

"What about him?"

"Ginny always sort of suggested that he was a really violent man. And he sure didn't like Ginny being with Tekla. Don't you think he might have wanted Tekla dead?"

"I do, yes. But how would he do it? They were around less than an hour when you were filling the tanks. Is there any way that someone could...I don't know...inject monoxide into a tank after it was filled?"

"No. Only through the compressor."

"So, same problem as with Sally. Motive, but no apparent opportunity."

"You sound like you do think it was my fault."

I threw myself back onto a pillow and closed my eyes. I didn't want to watch her face. "I don't believe for a second that you weren't filling those tanks properly, Jay. I don't believe you were negligent. But I'm no closer to knowing how else it could have happened, unless one tank did get switched by someone."

"Yeah." She came over and lay down. "Well, thanks for

trying."

"Hey, I'm not giving up. I will find out. But it's taking longer than I'd hoped. I'll go and talk to Pastor Dale tomorrow. I think catching him at the end of a church service should have him as off guard as possible." I rolled over and wrapped my arms around her. "I will find the truth of this, Jay. I just wish something would break before the trial."

* * *

Sunday morning, Jay insisted on staying in bed, eating peanut brittle washed down with champagne. She joked that she wanted to enjoy every luxury she could think of before it was too late. I went home for my gray skirt and jacket, then drove to the *Independent Children of Jesus Christ Evangelical Congregation* out in Metchosin where Ralph Dale was the pastor. I sat in the Mini across the road from the door and watched people go in. Most of the congregation were older, wearing hats, gloves, and suits ten to fifteen years out of date. They looked like tired people, I thought, not an eager, worshipping crowd like some churches had, but people who'd given up on most things and only worshipped out of duty or fear.

Reluctantly, I left the Mini and headed in. The sanctuary was only half full even though it was one minute to eleven. Mrs. Dale was pumping out wailing hymns from an old organ while the congregation stood waiting for the entrance of the choir and minister. I could see Ginny standing in the front row, right under the pulpit. When Ginny glanced briefly around I caught sight of an impressive shiner around her left eye. Obviously, Ginny must have gone home and received punishment for her sins, and now was here, dutifully worshipping at her judge's feet.

The choir loft doors opened and the choir, wearing threadbare maroon gowns with white collars, filed in. Ralph Dale strode in behind them and mounted his pulpit. His gown was deep purple, resplendent with gold trim—no fraying for the pastor.

"Glory be to the Father, and to the Son, and to the Holy Ghost," he intoned holding his hand up over the congregation.

"Holy, holy, holy," the congregation began singing back,

accompanied by the asthmatic organ. I remembered my childhood days in church pews and shivered. So many of the fundamentalist churches carried on their services the same way. I glanced at the church calendar. Yes, exactly the same sort of notices: women's circle, prayer meeting, ministerial counseling. That childhood feeling of steel bands tightening around me so I wouldn't say or do anything wrong came back. It felt hard to breathe.

After much singing and praying, Ralph Dale got down to the serious part of the morning, a hellfire and brimstone sermon, clearly directed at Ginny, about the eternal punishment that would befall women who strayed from the chaste path.

At last, the service was over. I hung back and watched people file out. Mrs. Dale came down and guided Ginny out through the choir loft doors. I noticed Ginny was limping, almost dragging her left leg. It looked like Ralph's punishment had got quite out of hand. I shivered.

Finally, as the last blue-rinsed, flower-hatted lady was shaking Ralph's hand, I walked toward him and started to introduce myself.

"I remember you," he interrupted. "One of those evil women who told my girl to defy me."

"Hardly. I just dived with her." I decided to go right to the point, no sense being tactful with this guy. "I want to know how you feel about your daughter's marriage to Tekla Takale?"

The man narrowed his eyes and stared at me. I felt as if he was attempting to send me to hellfire at that very moment just by the concentration of his will. His entire body seemed consumed with hatred as he looked at me. "Better to marry than to burn," he said finally, quoting Saint Paul.

"So you accept the marriage?" I asked, somewhat surprised.

He took a step closer, and at a good six foot two or three was as close as anyone comes to towering over me. I stepped back.

"My daughter is safe at home with me where she should be." He placed one hand on my shoulder and pushed me back into the door frame. He was strong and I was pinned before I could resist. "If I'd known one of you was in my Church, I'd have called down the Lord's punishment on you. The Lord will see that you don't live much longer. The evil ones, like you and that Takale fellow, always meet a just fate." He turned on his heel and stalked back through the sanctuary and through the choir loft door.

I watched him go. His rage at the world radiated around him like an aura. I couldn't imagine what must have happened to make him such an angry man. Certainly, he had the rage and holy righteousness to kill Tekla. I decided it was worth checking into his background. But where would a minister pick up knowledge about carbon monoxide and scuba tanks? Then I had a mental flash of Mrs. Dale driving the big motor home. She had worked in that garage and with the big eighteen-wheelers. For sure there would have been a compressor there. Jay might be right about Ralph's motive for killing Tekla after all. But could both the Dale Seniors be involved? I would have to find some way to check.

* * *

The remaining days until the trial passed too quickly and without the developments we wanted. Eva had asked to see the tanks and had looked at the one the tests found carbon monoxide in but she said it looked identical to the others, and the cops wouldn't let Jay check herself.

Meanwhile Jay and I spent time walking along the beaches of Victoria, me speculating about where the monoxide could possibly have come from, and Jay speculating about her possible sentence. But we spent more time in her condo holding each other, learning the tender geography of our bodies. Right then, the most important thing was to spend as much time in each other's arms as possible.

The day before the trial I scooted to my office to pick up some courtroom clothes, then headed to Jay's to pick her up for the trip to Anenome Island. Eva had arrived while I was away. Jay was dressed and had an overnight bag packed and set by the door. She was sitting at her desk staring across it, perfectly still.

"Hi," I said, trying to sound upbeat. "Are you two all ready to go?"

"As ready as we're going to be, it seems," Eva said.

"What does that mean?" I asked.

"It's going to be a rout," Eva replied. She gestured toward Jay. "She's a disaster as a witness. I can't put her on the stand or she'll be torn to shreds. And that means I've got no way to attack the statement."

"I'm just trying to tell the truth," Jay muttered.

"You're hanging yourself with your truth," Eva barked. "You've been filling tanks and running dives for ten years. Why can't you say you did everything normally, taking all the normal precautions and steps?"

"Because I don't know. I can't remember. If Pete really gave me as much vodka as he says he did, it's not much wonder I don't remember."

"That's not the point. We don't remember things that are habitual. That's why you have to stress how all the safety measures were habits you always carried out."

"But I can't swear to that."

"If you don't, you're going to prison. I can *swear* to that. So make up your mind, woman." Eva stalked out the door and roared away in her BMW.

I went over and kissed Jay on the cheek. "Come on, my love, we have to catch a ferry."

"Calliope," Jay took my hands and gripped tightly. "I've got no right to ask this, but...but I guess I'm going to jail. You heard Eva. I...I want to ask you to come and visit me. I know I can't ask you to wait until I get out; you're just too wonderful and loving a woman to be left alone for very long, but—"

"Of course, I'll visit," I said. "And I'll keep working on your case. There has to be something here that I'm missing. Both Sally and Ralph Dale have strong motives. And Ralph seems quite crazy. Even if we don't win this now, I will get you out soon. I promise you that."

Chapter Eleven

I woke in the darkness, and felt a sharp moment of crisis when I didn't know where I was. Then I remembered; we'd ferried to Anemone Island and were safely tucked in Faith's tower room, safe for now.... But Jay wasn't beside me.

"Jay, where are you?" I whispered

"Couldn't sleep." The answer came from the far side of the tower. I stared until I could make out her silhouette against the wall.

"Come and lie down. At least try to relax. I'll give you a massage."

"It's okay. It's already five. I'm wide awake."

"Come sit by me then."

Jay walked slowly toward the bed.

"What on earth are you doing? You're naked," I started to giggle as Jay passed through the faint light of the window. "You must be freezing. Get in here."

"Just trying to decide on my wardrobe. Do you think stripes are still in at your average prison?" Jay sat down, looked at me apparently seriously for a moment, then suddenly, jumped on top of me and began tickling under my arms.

I shrieked with surprise. "Stop that. Stop. We'll wake Faith."

Jay was laughing, gripping my wrists with one hand and

tickling with the other. "I want you to remember me. I want to make sure you remember me, no matter how long they send me away for. I'll tickle you mercilessly until you promise."

"I will. Promise," I giggled. "Let me up." I struggled to get free, but Jay scissored her legs around my waist and continued tickling. I had no chance against her strength.

"How are you going to like having a lover in prison? Maybe you can brag about how tough your prison moll is when you're out with your other women."

"Jay, stop it. This isn't going to help anything."

"Help what? I feel fine," she laughed, but her voice was shrill. "Might as well have some fun with this. Hey, I've never been to jail. I just realized I don't know a damn thing about it. Damn uneducated, you know. Maybe I'll learn something."

"Jay, let me go. I don't like this."

"What? Being held prisoner? I wonder if this is what it's like? Somebody holding you down and tickling you even when you don't like it. Come on, Cal, fight back, fight back."

I forced myself to go completely limp like I sometimes manage in meditation. I could still feel Jay's tickling, but my nerves didn't respond. Jay tickled harder and harder, then started shaking me. "Come on Cal, fight back, fight me. I need some practice if I'm gonna be tough girl on the cell block."

"No." I stayed limp, but gritted my teeth to avoid tears.

Jay rolled away. "You're no fun. Can't even try to laugh at myself with you around."

"That wasn't fun and you know it. Look, we've got four hours before we have to be in court. What do you want to do?"

"I don't know," Jay said more quietly. "It doesn't matter. I'm sorry I woke you. I just hadn't really thought about what was going to happen until last night. I was so upset about Tekla, I never really thought about...prison."

"Why don't you curl up and I'll hug you."

"Can't stay still." She bounded off the bed and half way across the room. "Wait a minute, I do know what I want to do. Let's go for a jog along the beach, in the fresh air. I might not be able to do that...much longer."

"Jog?" I repeated incredulously. Jay knows how I feel about jogging as far as the garage. "You really want me to jog?"

"Come on, Cal. You can do it. I've been secretly working you up to it with all the swimming and walking. Now you're going to have to do it...on your own for a while. Let's take this last chance. I can give you some pointers."

We jogged down Faith's block to the boardwalk and another two blocks along the sand before my legs were quivering. "Not another step," I gasped.

"Keep walking. Don't stop. You've got to cool down," Jay called back. "I'll be back in ten."

I watched as she streaked down the beach and disappeared. It was five minutes before I saw her clearly again, running back just as powerfully, just as fast.

"There, I'm fit for it. I can take whatever comes," Jay said, but she was shaking when she threw her arms around me. "Bring on the judge. Bring on the prison."

I took her face in my hands and kissed her, tasting salt on her lips. "Jay, I love you. And I'll keep loving you whatever happens. Don't forget that."

We walked slowly, me limping with a cramp in my calf, back to Faith's and showered. I went downstairs to drink cappuccino with Faith. It was a long time before Jay came down. When she did, all traces of bravado had disappeared. "Do you think I look all right?" she whispered. "Eva said I should look as professional as possible." She was wearing a tailored navy suit, white silk shirt, and low navy heels. Her hair was shining and she had put on the slightest touch of make-up.

"You look very professional. And beautiful as well, " Faith said.

I just nodded, afraid to speak, and took Jay's hand as we headed out the door.

* * *

Eva's predictions about the trial were accurate. The Crown Attorney, Edgar Coholly, carefully and precisely called his evidence: Dr. Binkley who did the autopsy; Peter Demchuk who testified to Jay's drunkenness and lack of interest in anything but him that night; the water properties expert who explained how quickly silt would settle around Tekla, and estimated that he must have been lying still on the bottom for ten to fifteen minutes for the water to clear. Corporal Hansen was called and entered Jay's statement into the record and insisted it had been made voluntarily, in midafternoon. Nothing Eva asked could shake him.

She had more success with the air quality analyst from Victoria who'd worked on the tanks. He testified that one of the tanks contained twenty-seven parts per million of carbon monoxide, not enough necessarily to kill anyone, at least not at the surface, though the effects under water pressure would increase. He also pointed out that the tanks had been refilled which would naturally dilute the concentration. Before she finished, Eva asked him about the other tanks.

"Did any of the other tanks have carbon monoxide in them?"

"No, the others were all perfectly pure."

"How do you explain that when two tanks were being filled at one time? Shouldn't there have been two tanks with monoxide traces?"

He had the good grace to hesitate at that, but not to give way. "Not necessarily. The other one may have been completely refilled such that no traces were left."

There was a recess when the Crown finished its case, and I joined Eva and Jay at the front of the courtroom.

"What do you think?" I asked.

"We're losing," Eva said simply. "The weakness in the tank evidence is helpful, but I don't think it's enough. Not with that damn statement." She turned to Jay. "It really is up to you now. If you want, I'll put you on the stand and we can try to negate the statement. But that means cross-examination. And Coholly over there is a real bastard when it comes to cross. What do you say?"

Jay took my hand. "Do you think I killed him? Be truthful."

"No. I've told you that, over and over."

"Then I'll fight. Put me on the stand Eva. I'll do my best."

"Good," Eva said. She leaned over and brushed a stray wisp of hair back from Jay's forehead. "Good luck," she smiled.

The Judge returned and the session began again. Eva led Jay through the story of her training, her ten year career, her careful habitual actions on the Saturday and Sunday in question. Eva asked her if she'd known about Peter's triple vodkas and Jay said that she had no idea. Then Eva started asking about the questioning in the Anemone Island cells. It was clear that Jay had very little idea when she had been questioned and when she had been left alone, but it was also clear that a lot of the questioning was done through the night.

"Why would they have kept questioning you through the night," Eva asked, "if they already had a signed statement?"

"Objection," called the Crown. "That calls for a conclusion of the witness."

"Objection sustained," said the Judge. But Eva smiled; she knew the point had been made.

"No more questions, your Honor," Eva said.

The cross examination began slowly. Coholly asked several questions about how many divers Jay had certified—over two thousand, how many accidents or close calls she'd had before—none. It seemed to be going well.

"Now tell me about your drinking on the Saturday night," Coholly asked.

"I didn't know I was drinking, not very much. I asked Pete for straight orange juice after the first one."

"And you couldn't tell the difference between triple vodkas and orange juice?"

"I didn't notice, no," said Jay.

"Come now," smiled Coholly. "Do you really mean to tell this court that at thirty-one years old, a smart independent woman like you doesn't notice when she's being served triples instead of virgin drinks?" He placed enough emphasis on the word *virgin* to make his innuendo clear.

"I don't normally drink much at all. I guess I'm not as experienced as some in that area," Jay replied, clipping the syllables precisely.

"And you didn't notice yourself feeling drunk?"

"No."

"Remarkable. What about Sunday morning? Why were you breathing pure oxygen from your resuscitator?"

"I was tired. I had a headache."

"You were hungover?"

"I didn't know that then."

"But it felt like it? Or are you going to tell us you've never had a hangover before?"

"Of course I have."

"And you knew just what to do, didn't you? Breathe some pure oxygen."

"Instructors do that sometimes. It gives you extra...zip."

"So there you were, feeling lousy enough to need oxygen, yet you still took these students out in the water, without apparently considering their safety with you in that condition?"

"That's ridiculous. I didn't feel that bad."

"Do you normally need a resuscitator in the morning?"

"Of course not."

"Thank you. I think that makes the point about how you were feeling." The audience laughed. Coholly consulted some notes. "Now tell me about this compressor," he asked.

I felt myself tense. His drinking questions had been bad enough, but this was the crucial area. If only Jay would answer strongly.

"Where was the compressor in relationship to your fire-side party?" he began.

"About fifty yards away, behind some trees."

"So you couldn't see it when you were dancing?"

"No, but I could hear it. And I know how it sounds when it's working properly. I would have noticed any change."

"Even as drunk as you were and over the noise of your dance music?"

"Yes."

"Remember you're under oath, Ms Campbell. Didn't you put the compressor there so that its noise wouldn't interfere with the party?"

"Yes, but—"

"Exactly. Now tell me, how did you make sure no monoxide went in through the air intake?" asked Coholly.

"I rigged the intake up a tree, high above the exhaust and away from it."

"In what direction from the exhaust was the air intake?"

Jay paused. "Higher up," she said finally.

"No, I mean what compass direction? East of the exhaust? West of it?"

I could see her stiffen and go pale, and I could tell she wouldn't be able to explain herself. "I always rig it up wind from the exhaust."

"And what direction was the wind coming from that Saturday night?" he paused. "I remind you again, Ms Campbell, you are under oath."

"I...don't remember," she said quietly.

"You did check that before rigging up the intake?"

"Yes."

"You're sure?"

"Look, checking the wind is a habit. I always do it. So yes, I did it that night."

"And how many times did you check the wind direction in the course of the evening?"

"I don't know."

"More than five times?"

"I said I don't know."

"Three times?"

"I don't know."

"Then I ask you again, did you ever check it, Ms Campbell?"

"I don't remember."

"So for five hours, you partied while the compressor chugged along on its own, and the wind could have been blowing exhaust into those tanks the whole time?"

"It obviously didn't or we'd all be dead."

"I'm asking for your sworn testimony about what you personally know. Now, knowing as you do that any exhaust in the tanks could be deadly to your students for whom you were totally responsible, did you ever check the wind direction to ensure that it wasn't blowing into the intake hose?"

"I don't know."

"In your *expert* opinion, can you think of any other way the carbon monoxide could get into Tekla Takale's tank?"

"Objection," Eva shouted. "That's calling for sheer speculation."

"I agree," said the Judge. "Objection sustained."

"No further questions," said Coholly, knowing that his point had been made as well.

Both Coholly and Eva made their final arguments then and the Judge called another recess before announcing his decision. Jay stood quietly at the defense desk and I came up to be with her.

"It's all over, isn't it?" said Jay.

"No," I said vehemently. "I'm going to keep on working. I'll find out what happened."

"We know what happened, Cal," said Jay. "That man's questions really showed it. I just have to face what comes now. I want you and Eva to take care of selling the store. Try to sell it to someone who wants to run a shop. That's better than having to sell off the inventory bit by bit. And then, whatever's left after the bills are paid, stick in the bank for me. I'll have it when I get out…to start…something new…" Jay shook her hair away from her face. "And please, come and see me. Oh god, I hope it isn't for too long…."

"I love you Jay," I whispered. "Of course I'll come to see you."

"Sorry to interrupt," Eva said, "but we need to decide what to do next. If he comes back with a guilty verdict, I can get an adjournment so we can bring some character witnesses in to speak to sentence. But that will mean staying in the lock-up here until the next court date, a month from now."

"No." Jay's face was paper white and taut with the effort she made to keep from shaking "Just get over it over with. I'm ready right now for whatever happens. No more limbo. I'll just have to wait for Cal to come up with something real, won't I?—if there is anything."

With that she turned her back on both of us and went back to her seat just as the Clerk of the Court announced, "The accused will rise to hear the verdict." I scurried back to my seat just as the Judge returned.

"Jennifer Campbell," the Judge said, "much of the evidence here is circumstantial. However, after considering it all, I'm left with no question in my mind that Tekla Takale's death, on Sunday April Twelfth, was due to your recklessness the evening before while filling the scuba tanks. Your conduct on that Saturday evening—drinking a great deal, partying through the night, putting the compressor and those life-giving tanks out of sight and, obviously, out of mind—was a marked, indeed an astonishing and wilful departure from the standard required in such a life-threatening business. Your conduct Sunday morning, taking students diving when you were badly hungover, was also a marked departure from the standards. Clearly, you were not able to keep track of their whereabouts.

"By now, you are no doubt aware that this is a crime that

does not demand any intention on the part of the accused, only wanton or reckless disregard of others' safety. I have no recourse then, but to find you guilty of criminal negligence causing death."

He turned to Eva. "Ms Nakolev, do you wish to bring evidence to sentence?"

"No Your Honor. My client wants to proceed to sentence immediately."

"Is that agreeable, Mr. Coholly?"

"Yes, Your Honor."

The Judge turned his attention back to Jay. "This is a major crime carrying with it a possible life sentence. However unintentional, you have caused the death of a person who trusted that you were caring for him. On the other hand, you have no previous record with the courts, and the evidence indicates that other than this one weekend you have probably been a fine and careful scuba instructor. Taking all of this into consideration, I am sentencing you to eighteen months to be served in a provincial correctional institution. Do you have anything to say?"

Jay shook her head. She was barely managing to hold herself standing.

"Bailiff, remove the prisoner. Court is adjourned."

I watched helplessly as Jay held out her wrists to accept the handcuffs the Bailiff held. She didn't turn once to look back at the courtroom as she was led away. I tried to breathe, but felt as if a huge rock had settled on my chest, suffocating me.

"What...what can we do now?" I muttered to Eva who was clattering angrily down the aisle.

"Not a damn thing. In fact, considering that cross-examination, she's lucky she didn't go down for longer. Judge Feldman is always sympathetic to pretty women, thank goodness."

"When can I see her?"

"They usually keep them without visitors for the first

while. Upsets the new prisoners too much, so they say."

"She'll need support."

"It's best to leave her alone."

"You must be joking. Right now, especially—"

"You have to understand, Cal, the system wants quiet prisoners with no sense that they have any rights. So they try to knock all their sense of self out in the beginning. She has to adjust and accept that. They use every technique going that's legal: fingerprinting, pictures with numbers, delousing, body searches. They'll take her clothes and put her in a uniform, keep her in a cell that's always lit and under surveillance. They'll march her around in single file with a hundred others once a day for exercise and three times a day to the cafeteria. Other than that, she'll be locked up by herself except for a few assessment sessions with the prison shrink. She won't be the same person when you see her again, Cal. I have to warn you of that."

"And if I find evidence showing that he was murdered?"

"Then maybe we can get her out. But the evidence has to be awfully compelling to make them do that once a verdict has been rendered."

"It will be, damn it. I just have to find it." I dropped back down on the courtroom bench. "I'm not much help to my friends."

"You did what you could. Come on," said Eva. "Get up now and go back to Faith's. Spend the night there and then come back into town and back into the world. Jay has to face her future by herself with whatever strength she can find. Without dreams of some new miracle evidence."

"It's not fair," I insisted.

"Calliope," said Eva sternly. "It is fair. I have to tell you that given the evidence, there's no question in my mind that Tekla died because of Jay's negligence. It's time you accepted that. Now, I'll arrange to have the tanks and compressor sent back to the shop so we can inventory them, and I'll start advertising the shop. The sooner we can sell it, the better it'll be for her."

I drove slowly back to Faith's, concentrating as hard as I could on noticing the little bumps and holes in the road, not thinking. Faith was waiting in the living room.

"I can tell by your face," Faith said. She jumped up and hugged me. "It was terrible. Sit down, have some cognac, and then talk."

"Nothing much to tell. The police had no new evidence. But the question of how that monoxide got in there was the deciding factor."

"How long, Cal?"

"Eighteen months."

"Oh," Faith smiled a small smile. "Well, I know that's not good, but it could have been much worse. You don't know yet, Cal, but eighteen months isn't very long in a whole life-time. And besides there are all the early release programs. She could be back with us in six months. Why, we may even be able to save her store for her."

"What?"

"Well, I was thinking this afternoon that maybe I should buy the store. Diversify my investments, you know. I could hire Janeen to run it. She's desperate to get away from that janitorial firm. Of course, we'd have to hire an instructor to do the teaching."

I took a sip of brandy. I knew Faith felt as helpless as I did and was stretching for any comfort. "I don't know, Faith. There's no way of knowing if Jay will feel like running the store when she gets out. And she won't be able to teach again."

"And what about if she is vindicated—if you finally find the evidence that will acquit her? If we can keep it for her, she'll have the choice of being there."

"True. It's a very kind idea."

"It's practical. She's built a very sound business I discovered when I talked to the banks. So, tomorrow, when you get back to Victoria, I want you to talk with that lawyer woman and have her start arranging the sale. I want everything done properly so it's clear that this is a real sale, not just a *kind idea*. I may be an old lady, but I intend to keep making money. And I want clear job security for Janeen. I can't offer her a job for six or eighteen months and then expect her to disappear when Jay gets out. I expect to expand the shop and make it a major paying proposition. When Jay gets out, she and I can negotiate how she gets back into the business if she wants to."

Chapter Twelve

Tuesday morning on my way back to Victoria, I couldn't even work up the enthusiasm to indulge in my usual race against traffic in the Mini from the ferry to my apartment. Consequently, the drive took fifteen minutes longer than usual. The phone answering machine was blinking furiously and I considered hurling it into the wastebasket. Instead I ignored it and headed through to the bathroom for a jacuzzi. Jay's blue sweats were hanging on the back of the door, and I had to struggle to keep my composure when I saw them. Oh my love, I thought, forgive me for failing you. I took the sweats, folded them compulsively until they looked as if they came straight from the store, then put them in my bottom drawer. They'd be there for her. "I won't stop trying to find what really happened, my love," I whispered, "even if everyone else is accepting this thing as over and done with."

Once sunk in the jacuzzi, I let the hot bubbles tingle against my back and tried to relax. Next to yoga and meditation, the jacuzzi was the only thing that could ever unwind my wound-tight muscles. Trapezoids relax, I ordered, deltoids relax. Breathe in, hold it, exhale and relax. But this time nothing worked. I couldn't concentrate through three breaths before my mind was back ruminating over the events since the death. Something Nazki had said bothered me. I tried to run my brain stylus through the wrinkles, but I couldn't place the problem. There was just an uneasy feeling that I should have questioned something more than I did.

I dragged myself out of the jacuzzi five minutes before the bubbles were timed to stop, dressed, and headed for the office. I had to find Nazki and talk again. With luck, that would stimulate my memory.

As I reached for the phone, it rang. It was Danielle, and she had lost her usual school teacher's calm.

"I've been phoning and phoning you. Don't you return your messages?"

"I just got home from the trial."

"Sally's disappeared."

"What?"

"She's gone. She's been terribly upset ever since you and Jay were here. Two nights ago she said she needed to go for a drive by herself. She hasn't come back."

"What does that suggest to you?" I asked harshly.

"Nothing, except that she has such awful memories from that time."

"It suggests guilt to me; flight usually does."

"Look Cal, I've only known Sally for seven months, and I admit, she has some problems. But she would never kill anyone. I know that. Please, Cal, you've been my friend forever. Help me find her."

"Even if I'm looking for different reasons?"

"You'll see that I'm right."

"I'll be at your place in half an hour."

Before leaving the apartment, I phoned Janeen, told her about Faith's idea for the shop, convinced her that she should be the one to finish the inventory, and asked her to phone the airports, bus terminals, ferries, police, motels, and hospitals, all within a hundred mile radius to see if she could find a trace of Sally. I knew Janeen would think up stories compelling enough that the authorities would give her information if there was any to be had. I'd used her as an assistant before in cases and knew how sharp she was.

Then I headed for Dani's. When she answered the door, I was shocked. Her right jaw was purple and swollen.

"Sally?" I asked.

Her embarrassed look answered in the positive, even as she shook her head.

"Bloody hell, Dani. It's a good thing she ran off or I'd kill her."

"You don't understand. She was terribly upset. We got in a row about openness with each other. I pushed too hard."

"She hit you, Dani. Wake up. Abuse isn't okay just because it comes from a woman."

"Her precious father, who she still idolizes, used to beat her and her brother silly. This has only happened once before, and we've been working on it. Everything was going well."

"Dani, that's nuts. You should have thrown her out the minute it happened the first time."

"No. I love her and I was helping her. She was getting calmer and really open about her feelings. Then you had to remind her of that awful time in Ethiopia. Please, help me find her."

"Oh, you bet I'll help."

We headed out and began checking Sally's customary haunts: a cappuccino bar on Blanshard, the Odeon Cinema.... Dani brought a photograph, but no one had seen her. We'd been hunting for about an hour when my cellular rang. It was Janeen.

"I think I've found her," Janeen said. "That Jaguar of hers is a dead give away. I decided to start with gas stations and found a guy at a Save-on Gas, just north of Nanaimo up the coast highway, who remembered the Jag from late Saturday night. So I phoned motels in that area hoping she'd got tired and stopped. Well, turns out, she's still there. At least the Jag is. She checked in with a Visa card, so she obviously isn't trying to hide. She told them she might stay a few days, so they haven't bothered to see if she's still there."

"Name?"

"Dew Drop Inn. Can you believe that!"

"Thanks Jan. You're brilliant at this, you know. Too bad I can't hire you full time."

"Too bad you don't work for money full time," Janeen laughed. "Maybe soon I'll be able to hire you...at the dive shop. Take care."

It took ninety minutes for the Mini to eat up the miles between Dani's house and the Dew Drop Inn. We parked beside Sally's white Jag and knocked at Unit three.

"Who is it?" It was Sally's voice.

"Sally, it's me," called Dani. "Let me in."

"Go away, Dani. You shouldn't have tried to find me. It's no good. I can't see you. I'm going away."

"I'm here too," I said. "Jay's been sent to jail for eighteen months, and I'm not letting you go anywhere. So you can open up to us or I'll call the cops."

We could hear a chain being drawn out of the lock and the deadbolt turning. The door swung open and we followed Sally's back into the 1950s-tacky motel room. One table lamp lit the double bed and the gold framed picture of mountain-sunset-with-wild-horse that hung above it.

"So, what's the story?" I asked. "Why did you run?"

"To think."

"Oh sure."

"Damn it, Cal," interrupted Dani. "Don't."

"It's all right, Dani," said Sally. "She's got good reasons."

"So, what's the story?" I repeated.

Sally sat down on the bed and stared into the floor. She spoke so quietly I had to kneel down in front of her, getting my ear as close to her voice as possible. "I did take the bribes in Ethiopia." She glanced at Dani who had kneeled beside me. "Damn it Dani, I'm sorry, but it's true."

"Thirteen thousand dollars worth?" I asked, surprised because I'd actually believed her story of the set-up.

"Certain businessmen gave me money for drugs, then sold them on the blackmarket. In turn they encouraged villagers to use the clinic. Tekla convinced me that bribery was so much a part of life there that people wouldn't trust me if I didn't take bribes. Ironic, eh? I guess that's how he kept everyone in line. He always had some hold on each of us." She paused. "I was young then, and stupid, and made some very bad decisions. I prayed that nobody here would ever find out about it. But here we are," she paused again. "I'll understand, Danielle, if you never speak to me again."

"I can't believe it! I thought you were... hell, I thought I was a good judge of character. I suppose Cal was right and you made up the rape story when the truth is you simply got caught taking bribes, right?" asked Dani.

"The rape really happened. But I did get caught taking bribes. That really happened too."

"How could you be so...." Danielle paused.

"Dishonest? Immoral? I don't know. I've had ten very long years to wonder that, but I still don't have any good answers. I...I seem to have a...a kind of black hole inside that I fall into when things go wrong. I'm sorry."

Dani walked over to the window and stared out, her back rigid against the room.

"So what did Tekla want you to do for him here?" I asked.

"What do you mean?"

"Don't play dumb. I don't want to hurt you, Sally. But I'm not going to let Jay down. I'll bet I can find records of this Ethiopian story. And I'll use them if you don't help me all you can. Now tell me, what did Tekla want?"

"Free counseling."

"About what?"

"That's confidential, I already told you."

"I don't give a flying fig if it's confidential. Right now, you're my prize suspect for a murder. So you'd better talk to me unless you want me going to the cops with your background."

Sally stared into her hands and said nothing until Dani whirled around and grabbed Sally by the shoulders, and started to shake her. "For god's sake tell her about it. Tell us you aren't a murderer, damn it."

I laid my hand gently on Dani's arm to stop the shaking. She stepped back and grabbed my hand tight. The two of us watched Sally shake her head back and forth, as if fighting with herself.

Finally she started, "You know, fifteen years ago, at my folks' place, a bat came down the chimney into this round fireplace they had. It was a common problem in the area, but this bat was trying to wiggle its way out, and I could see it was going to succeed and be flying around the house any minute. I was home alone and terrified. I'd always heard that bats carried rabies so I was afraid to try to catch it. I'd also heard that you could build a small fire under them and they'd fly back up the chimney. So I built a fire—just six or eight little twigs. But the bat didn't fly up, it fell into the fire. I can still hear that damn thing screaming. It haunts me in nightmares. How the hell do you think I could murder somebody?" She looked straight up at me then, and I could see the horror in her eyes.

"Okay, Sally. But please, tell me what you know about Tekla. Jay needs your help," I said.

"He was sort of like that bat. A person perfectly suited to do what he wanted to do, which was rule Ethiopia. He was part of Haile Selassie's family, and..."

"I've heard that part from Nazki."

"Yeah, well, he was intelligent, a brilliant organizer, and expected to be obeyed. But he felt out of place here. And his mind was full of the oddest combination of rigorous western science and his home country superstitions. He came to me because he was convinced someone was trying to kill him using the evil eye."

"You're kidding?"

"No. Belief in the evil eye isn't at all unusual—all around the Mediterranean and eastern Africa. Italy's one of the worst places. But it's common in Ethiopia—oddly enough, the

Christians, like Tekla, all believe the Moslems can give them the evil eye and vice versa."

"Gosh, I love religion."

"Yeah."

"So what made him think someone here was doing it?"

"He thought it was someone from Ethiopia sending this energy all the way here. And he firmly believed he was dying. He had headaches all the time, and felt as if his energy was being drained. I tried to get him to eat better. He was stuck on a diet of rice and peppers, tasty but insufficient. And I also offered to do some medical tests, but he wasn't much interested in those. The other thing was he kept finding little evil eye charms in his briefcase, in his carrel in the library, everywhere he went. A stone, a twist of hair…. That part was eerie."

"The stone on the dive," I realized.

"What stone?"

I explained, "When they got him to the hospital and unclenched his hand, he was holding a stone with an eye painted on it."

Sally shuddered. "Oh god. I told him he shouldn't worry about it."

"That's reasonable enough. How could a stone kill him?"

"He was so frightened. I couldn't help but feel sorry for him. He knew he had enemies."

"What about Nazki? Do you think he had anything to do with this evil eye business? He had easy access."

"I suggested that to Tekla. But he didn't think so. He said Naz was his best friend, and totally apolitical. But Nazki is an obvious suspect it seems to me."

"Why?"

"Because he's from Eritrea."

"So?"

"Cal, the Eritreans have been fighting for their independence against the central government since the '60s. They fought Haile Selassie for decades, and now they're fighting the military council. I always thought it was odd that Naz would even speak to someone like the royal heir."

"So they're from enemy groups?"

"Absolutely. It was Tekla's great family that annexed—that's the polite word—Eritrea into Ethiopia. Naz should have hated him. And, Naz is Moslem. He'd be a perfect one to give Tekla the evil eye."

Not for the first time, I cursed my limited knowledge about world events. "I need to spend more time with Nazki," I admitted. "Look, Sally, I want to believe you had nothing to do with Tekla's death. I certainly don't know how you could have got that monoxide in Tekla's tank. Come with me to confront Nazki. I'll forget about your Ethiopian problems unless we eliminate every other suspect, okay?"

"Thanks. How do you think Naz could have engineered Tekla's death?"

"I don't know, but he was Tekla's buddy. And we never have figured out how so much time lapsed between when Nazki says Tekla disappeared and when we found him."

"I really want to help Jay. I can't believe they convicted her. Is she going to appeal?"

"I doubt it. Eva thinks she was lucky as it is…So, will you follow us back to town in your Jag?"

"I'll go with Sally," said Dani quietly. "I think we have some things we need to talk about."

"Just make sure you come straight to my office," I said. "I'll expect you in an hour and a half."

* * *

By the time Sally rang the buzzer to the apartment, I had talked to Nazki. He tried three different reasons why he couldn't meet me, but I had kept at him until he agreed to see us at the co-op in half an hour. I also listened to my phone messages and called two potential clients to arrange interviews for the next morning.

Sally was by herself when I answered the door. "Dani's taken the Jag back to the house. If you could give me a ride there after we talk to Nazki, I'd really appreciate it."

"Sure," I agreed, then added, "I'm sorry all this had to come out in front of Dani. I didn't intend to create such havoc in your life."

"I created my own havoc, Cal. I've always known somehow that this would come out again. But Dani says I should stay with her for now anyhow. She says she has to think about what all this means to...to us, and to our plans about Guatemala. At least she hasn't thrown me out."

"I'm glad. I know she takes her third world ethics seriously."

"So do I, Cal," Sally said. "Believe it or not."

"I can tell from seeing your pain. But I have to do whatever's best for Jay, understand?"

Sally stared down at her feet but nodded yes.

"So let's go. I want to start the questioning when we see Nazki. But if he says anything that doesn't ring true, whether it's because of your knowledge of Ethiopia or of Tekla, then say so, right away. Okay?"

"Okay. Listen, one other thing, I guess I should tell you."

I waited.

She continued, obviously uncomfortable. "He wanted me to do an abortion, secretly, without making any records or anything. There was to be no trace."

"On who?"

"He didn't say."

"What did you say?"

"I agreed. I...I didn't know what else to do. It was only the lack of records that would be illegal."

"When did he ask?"

"Two weeks before the dive weekend."

"And when was it supposed to happen?"

"He said he'd tell me that later."

"Do you think it was for Ginny?" I wondered aloud.

"I thought about her. But I don't know. She's so uptight and afraid of her father, I'd expect her to be a virgin when she's fifty. And besides her mother's a hard core anti-abortion crusader. I've had her throw rotten eggs at me many a time. She's a real fanatic."

"I guess there are other ways of finding that out," I said. "Do you suppose that's why he and Ginny got married, because she was pregnant?"

"Maybe. I've also thought that might give Ralph Dale an even stronger motive to want to kill Tekla, if he found out somehow that Ginny was pregnant."

"Good point. The only problem is, I still can't figure out how someone else could have got the carbon monoxide in the tank."

"Couldn't Dale have come back while we were dancing and moved the air intake?"

"Possibly. But that would be taking a huge chance. How would he know Tekla would get the right tank? Come to think of it, how would anyone know that? Damn it," I exploded, "the more I think about it, the more the circumstances seem accidental, but the more I hear about Tekla, the more people I can imagine murdering him."

* * *

When we arrived at Nazki's room, it was clear that his reluctance on the phone had been overcome. He had a bottle of red wine opened and cheese and crackers set out on the table. "Thought I should have something to welcome you properly," he laughed. "The last time you saw this room, it was a shambles."

"This isn't a social visit, Naz," I said. "Though I must admit a glass of wine is tempting. You've fixed the room up nicely."

"The Manager helped me pack all of Tekla's belongings in some boxes and put them in the basement. I'm not quite sure where we should send them."

"I suppose to Ginny, if she wants them. By the way, did you happen to find their marriage certificate among the papers?"

"No. Nothing like that."

"I wonder if that's what the break-in was for," said Sally. "Suppose Mr. Dale wanted to erase all traces that Ginny and Tekla were connected, for instance. Or Peter," she added. "He wouldn't like that marriage much."

"Possible," I said. Sally was no slouch when it came to thinking up motives. "There'll be a record of it somewhere though." Still, I realized, I shouldn't forget Peter. He sure didn't like Tekla. And he did have easy access to Tekla's room. Then I remembered that Ginny had been there when the break-in was discovered. Could she have wanted something of Tekla's? And if so, what?

"I still can't see those two together," laughed Nazki. "Can you picture Empress Ginny of Ethiopia?"

"Hardly," I laughed. "Anyhow, I've got a few questions. How long have you been Tekla's friend?"

"Since London. We met in grad school five years ago."

"How did you happen to make friends with him when you were from an enemy group?"

Nazki laughed. "Ah, the good doctor's been giving you lessons in basic Ethiopian politics."

"Yes."

"Like I said, foreign students have to make what friends they can. I didn't care who he was."

"Had any of your friends or family been involved in the liberation movements?" Sally asked.

"Of course."

"Were any killed or injured?" she continued.

"Look, my friends and family include half of Eritrea if you count all the Beni Amer, so some of them must have been killed or injured."

"You must have hated Tekla and what he stood for." I said, following her line.

"No. I hate a system that makes people become enemies on the basis of where they were born. I refuse to get pulled into that bullshit. Sorry, no motive from that direction," he said and grinned.

My intuition, the sick feeling in my gut, told me there was still something I was missing, some important detail I wasn't picking up on, but I couldn't quite grasp it. Nazki had to be lying. When you grow up with those kinds of hatreds, you can't just dismiss them intellectually, at least not as easily as Nazki was suggesting. They stick in your heart. But I had no way to break through his apparent calm and rationality.

"What do you know about the evil eye?" Sally asked.

Nazki exploded into laughter, spraying wine as he did so. "What the hell? That's just superstition."

"Apparently Tekla believed in it," I said. "He went to Sally about it for help."

"You must be joking," said Nazki.

"No. He seriously thought someone was trying to kill him," said Sally.

"Don't believe it. He was putting you on. What else was he trying to get from you?" asked Nazki.

Sally's face paled, but she went on. "He seemed to think he needed medical help. Do you know why he'd think that?"

"No idea."

"After Tekla disappeared from your side, how long did you wait before coming and telling Jay?" I asked, deciding to try a different tack.

"I went right away. Jay trained us well. It never occurred to me not to tell her instantly."

"That's ironic," I growled, then lapsed into silence. I was no further ahead. "Okay, I guess I'll take you home, Sally. There's certainly nothing here that helps explain how Tekla died," I said. I wanted to allay any fears Nazki might have. He was just too cool about the whole thing. My intuition told me he had something to do with the death, though I had no idea of what. Unfortunately I had even less idea of how to figure it out. Maybe I should take everybody's advice and do some paying work for a change.

Chapter Thirteen

The next morning, I interviewed the two potential clients and accepted both jobs. Maybe being busy on other things would help my brain processes. And the money certainly wouldn't hurt. Besides the first would be a snap, a simple case of an adopted child looking for birth parents. I'd sort of specialized in these cases—they often had happy endings— so by now I'd developed a 'deep throat' within the Vital Statistics registry who would give me what I wanted quickly. A couple of phone calls would probably earn me the five-hundred dollar retainer I'd asked for. The other would be more difficult; an employee of a gemstone and jewelry store had gone missing along with the contents of the safe and a selection of the most expensive rings. It should be a job for the police, but the employee was the nephew of the owner.

"We're trying to help Philip find his proper place in the world," crooned Saul Taratsky, the owner. "We've hunted for him ourselves for a week now, but he's disappeared. We heard that you can find people and things quietly, without alerting the authorities. I will pay a great deal for the quiet return of my sister's boy."

I requested two thousand dollars up front from Mr. Taratsky, and asked him for photos of Philip and the missing jewelry. I didn't kid him either about the chances of success, but Taratsky was determined I should try. With the two retainer cheques all ready to be banked, I had expenses covered for a month or so. I should have felt elated but I didn't.

I picked up the phone to call the Department of Vital Statistics, but found myself dialing Dani's number instead. "Where would I go to find good info about the Ethiopian-Eritrean battles?" I asked when Sally answered. "I'm real suspicious of Nazki and I want to know more."

"It's not easy. Our papers don't follow those things in detail. You could try at the International Learner Center. They have a pretty good library."

"Where's that?"

"You sure are insular, Cal, aren't you?" Sally laughed. "I'll take you if you want. I've used the library a lot, boning up on the Guatemalan situation."

Half an hour later, I climbed into Sally's Jag and we headed for the Learner Center. I settled back into the soft leather and couldn't help but rub my finger along the sheen of the walnut dash. "This is one classy car. I could live in these seats."

"Yeah," Sally laughed. " I can't drive it above fifty and I count my mechanic among my closest friends, but I love it. It's so elegant. I'm going to have to sell it though...if we still go to Guatemala...."

"You certainly do want to go to that little jungle clinic, don't you?"

"Yeah, I do. My heart's always been in third world medicine. My dad practiced in China during the Long March and trained some of the barefoot doctors with Bethune. I always wanted to be like him."

"Yeah, I heard about him," I blurted angrily.

"What does that mean?"

"Dani says he beat you—must be hereditary; I saw the bruise on her jaw. I guess I should tell you that if I ever hear that you hit her again, I'll...."

Tires screeched as Sally wrenched the Jag across two lanes of traffic and into a parking lot. She stalled the engine and dropped her face into her hands; her whole body shook. I was shaking too but that was because she'd just about got me killed.

"You seem destined to find out all the worst things about me," she said finally, tears streaking her face. "What else did Dani tell you about me?"

"Only that you hit her but were 'working' on it."

"It's not an excuse but my Dad was a lot like Ginny's, a missionary doctor who thought he could punish the world on God's behalf. He did beat me—I'll spare you the boring details, but it happened often. I left home at sixteen, two days after killing the bat. Somehow I knew I'd gotten screwed up and needed to get away quick if I were going to stay sane."

"I'm sorry, Sally, but it's still no excuse for hitting Dani."

"I told her I'd leave. I don't deserve someone like her. But she has incredible faith in me. I...I promised to go to therapy but the shrink I chose has a six month waiting list. She gave me some books to read in the meantime."

I gulped and reassessed my feelings about Sally, saying in all honesty, "I hope it works for you."

"I'm doing my best, Cal, which isn't always very good, but I'm trying."

"How'd you ever get from teenage runaway to family doctor?"

"I went to live with my high school biology teacher and his wife. They watched out for me right through internship. They were so hurt when I moved here but I just couldn't face them after Ethiopia.... They were my only real family.... Is there anything else you want to know?"

I shook my head. "I was worried about Dani—"

"I know. She's told me how far you go back. Come on—we can walk from here."

Soon we climbed a rickety flight of back stairs to the second floor and went in. The office was decorated in the finest peeling yellow paint and army surplus filing cabinets. Not promising, I thought.

"They put all their money into getting and giving out

information. They don't care about the furnishings," said Sally apparently reading my thoughts.

"More power to them."

A tousle-haired red-head, who looked about eighteen years -old, came out of another room. "Hi Sally," he called. "What can I do for you?"

"Cal, this is Mike, the director of the Center," Sally introduced us. "Eritrea—do you have anything about the struggle for the last twenty or so years?"

"Yeah, lots. We had a volunteer, Zena Mohammed. She fled Eritrea, but she used to get a lot of papers and letters from home. She brought them all here. Her people were part of the resistance, you know, and she wanted the world to know about them." Mike spoke as he took folders from the nearest filing cabinet and piled them on a long table where we sat down. "There's a whole filing cabinet of clippings going back to '62 when Eritrea was annexed. It's all yours."

"Let's start at the most recent and work back," I said and dug in. At least this was what I was most familiar with, plowing through documents to find little clues, not badgering people about their miserable pasts. Maybe I'd be more successful here. As the hours passed, however, I learned more than I wanted to know about the Lion of Judah— another name for Haile Selassie; the Eritrean Liberation Front, which was the oldest group and mainly Moslem; the Eritrean People's Liberation Front, which was more recent, mainly Christian, and vying for power with the ELF; and even the Eritrean Women's Front which was apparently as militant as either of the men's groups. I found nothing I could use to tackle Nazki's calm facade. But I was more sure than ever that it was a facade.

Suddenly, Sally gave a small yelp and dropped the file she was carrying.

"What did you find?"

"Is this what you really wanted?" she asked. She handed over a crinkly clipping from *The Addis Ababa Observer*, January 27, 1982. It showed a younger, frightened-looking

Sally being escorted by two Ethiopian soldiers to a waiting plane. "Canadian doctor deported in bribery scandal" read the headline. I skimmed the article quickly and handed it back. "No, I didn't come for that. There's nothing there you haven't told me."

"Hey, that's right. I remember seeing that when I filed this stuff last year," said Mike as he came up behind our table. "What the hell happened?"

"I...uh...." Sally froze.

"She tried to report the boss for rape," I took over.

"That would do it. You have to be so careful. Things do get planted on people." He wandered back to the clippings he'd been filing. "Are you finding anything useful?"

"Not yet," I said. "I'm looking for information that would connect a young man here with any of the Eritrean freedom fighters or the anti-Selassie forces."

"I've got a file full of pictures of rebels and government fighters from various newspapers and other sources Zena wouldn't tell me about. That might be quicker."

"Let's have it."

"Coming right up," Mike said and headed through a door into another storage room.

"Thanks," Sally whispered to me. "I didn't know what to say."

"You don't have to wear that story round your neck like an albatross. It's over. Forget it."

"It's never over. I...."

"Here's your file, or files to be more accurate." Mike had reappeared by our side with a cardboard carton full of manila envelopes. "I'd forgotten we had so much."

It was another three quarters of an hour before I found it. "Bingo," I shouted. "I knew he was lying. I knew it." I had a copy of a news photo dated September 1973. It showed a white robed woman, face distorted with grief, holding the hands of two children, a boy who looked about eight and a girl who might have been four. The article below read *Saba Kiflu, wife of the second-in-command of the ELF guerrilla forces, with her children, Nazki and Najilah, at the funeral of her husband and their father, Nathar Kiflu, who was publicly hung in Asmara on the personal order of Emperor Haile Selassie. Widow Saba has sworn that she and her children will avenge his assassination.*

"Wow," said Sally, "Nazki must have been the one, don't you think?"

"It's looking more and more likely. I'll take a copy of this picture, but I need to figure out how he did it before I confront him."

Sally drove me back to the office. "Is there anything else I can do?"

"I'll call if there is. One question still puzzles me—what do you think Tekla saw in Ginny? As Nazki said, she's hardly a perfect wife for an Emperor."

"Who knows? A tiny conquest, I suppose. And Ginny is cute and funny—I imagine she makes a great date. I doubt if he intended to take her to Ethiopia though."

"My feeling too. I think I need to talk to Ginny again before I tackle Naz. I just have a feeling that something's wrong in her story."

When Sally dropped me at my office, I intended to phone Ginny and make an immediate appointment. However, the answering machine was flashing double numbers, so I felt duty-bound to listen. Three messages were from Janeen at the scuba shop urging me to phone her right away. One was from Saul Taratsky, also urging me to phone him instantly. He'd found photos for me and wanted to bring them right over. I phoned Janeen.

"I've got news," she said. "Good news, I think, though you're going to kick yourself when you hear it, Cal."

"You mean you've discovered something obvious that I didn't?"

"I think so."

"What?"

"An extra scuba tank."

"What!?" I choked, trying to contain my relief.

"An *extra* tank. When I inventoried the tanks released by

the police with those in her stock, there were fifty-one. That seemed like an odd number, so I phoned Jay's bookkeeper. She confirmed that Jay refused to keep any records saying the business was small enough to keep in one good head, but she knew Jay only had fifty tanks because they were new this year, and she had the list of serial numbers from the manufacturer. We checked them all out and guess what? Tank number fifty-one, the one with the odd serial number, also happens to be Exhibit One, the tank that tested positive for monoxide."

"Jan, you're a genius!"

"No, just a plodding researcher who is ever so pleased to be able to assist your own genius," Janeen teased. "So, you're coming right down to see this?"

"You bet. This will get Jay out."

"Let's hope, but—"

"I'll be right there."

I jumped in the Mini and sped toward the scuba shop. At the last minute, I circled back past Eva's office. The light was on. I buzzed the intercom and she let me in. There was a policewoman in her office, but she slipped out as I entered.

"So what do you think?" I asked after explaining about the extra tank. "Is that enough to go to the Crown with?"

"For what?" Eva asked.

"To get Jay out, for another trial maybe?"

"You must be joking. So there's an extra tank. You may know that but Coholly would just laugh. Knowing and proving are two different things."

"Okay, but I should go and see her right away then to find out if it was hers or not. And maybe she'll remember who helped Tekla with his equipment that morning."

"Sit down, Cal," Eva said, "and listen. I told you before it's time for you to accept the inevitable. The court has made its decision. An extra tank is not grounds for appeal. And even Jay agrees that the death was her fault. You're not doing her any favors going in with these little clues, raising her hope without any real substance."

"Even with this new evidence, something we even speculated about?"

"It's a start"

"So what would you do?"

"Cal, you love her, don't you?"

I stared at Eva. "What? It's written on my forehead?"

"Not at all. But I'm a lesbian too. So I recognize the signs." She motioned toward the exit. "My Mary's a police officer. Can you imagine a more horrible combination, a defense lawyer and a cop? You can understand why we stay pretty far inside our closet. I tell you, sometimes I could murder her, but the truth is she's the one who convinced me to go to law school."

I laughed, then sobered. "So what does she think about Jay's conviction?"

"She agrees that Jay's own testimony did her in."

"But what about getting her out?"

"Cal, just remember the Crown isn't going to budge now unless you can give him the whole package: motive, means, and murderer."

"Shit," I said. "Well, I want to see Jay as soon as possible anyhow. I do need to ask her some questions. I'm betting it was Nazki who helped Tekla put his equipment together; buddies always do. And Nazki had some compelling reasons to dislike his buddy."

"Interesting, but not conclusive of anything."

"All right, all right. But what about getting me into the jail?"

"They have good reasons for keeping visitors away during the adjustment period."

"So you've said. How soon?"

"I'll phone my contacts tomorrow and see what I can do."

Chapter Fourteen

I arrived at the scuba shop feeling depressed. "I talked to Eva," I told Janeen. "She doesn't think this extra tank means a damn thing, or not enough to do anything."

"You did leap to a few conclusions, Cal."

"The hell I did."

"Don't snap at me, Ms. Smarty Detective. I found the damn tank."

"Sorry Jan. I just...."

"You're just all emotionally wrapped up in this one. Too emotionally wrapped up. You're darting off in all directions. Not thinking with your usual clarity."

"The hell I'm not." I flopped down on the wooden chair beside the row of tanks. "You're right. What do you suggest?"

"Jay needs you to find out what happened. But you need to go back to what you do best."

"Such as?"

"Dull, boring, nitty-gritty research."

"On what? I feel like I'm at a dead end. I know Nazki's motive, but...."

"You really aren't thinking well, are you? On this tank. Where it came from and who brought it?"

"Of course. I'm just so damn...dispirited...."

"Come on, Cal. We're beginning to make progress. You need to check all the other scuba shops. Once we trace it, we'll have your means, I'm willing to bet on it."

I smiled at Janeen, recognizing her warm, encouraging words as those of a great friend. "I'll get started tomorrow."

"We already started," Janeen said. "I phoned the metro library. They're faxing me copies of the yellow pages for all the diving businesses in the region, one-hundred-mile radius. They should be all here by morning."

"Thanks Jan," I said quietly. "I'm sorry I snapped at you."

"I guess I could overlook that bit of temper. Especially if you buy me supper and a couple of stiff drinks before I go to work tonight. I got shifted back to the Mercantile Building by that supervisor who hates me. That damn building has the dirtiest toilets in this city. I swear they make mud pies in them."

* * *

I intended to be at the dive shop by nine the next morning to start making phone calls, but Saul Taratsky was on my doorstep by 8:30, and spent an hour and a half showing me the family photo album with pictures of sweet little Philip from the time he was a baby, as well as an album of jewelry designs. Evidently Taratsky Goldsmithing specialized in designs crafted for people of different cultural and religious backgrounds. There were filigreed gold crosses for Orthodox Christians, menorahs for Orthodox Jews, one ring with a little gold frog made for a woman who believed the frog was her spirit guide, even a gold labrys pendant and a ring with a double female symbol on it that I was pleased to see. At another time, I would have been fascinated by the jewelry. I admire beautiful jewelry, even though I don't have any except a locket that holds Liz's picture, a locket I'll never be able to wear again. But that morning, all I wanted was to send Taratsky on his way. It was 10:30 before I got to the shop. Janeen was already there and phoning.

"You're burning the candle at both ends, aren't you?" I asked. "When did you get off work?"

"I finished about two million toilets around 3 a.m.

Couldn't sleep so I came down here and did some more inventory."

"I'd think you didn't want to run this store, the way you're working to find evidence for Jay."

"Don't joke, Cal." Jan's tone was suddenly serious. "I love working here already. And I had the great pleasure of giving my worm of a boss my notice last night. But I want to see Jay out of that prison as soon as possible. It's not good for a person."

"Your husband did time, didn't he?"

"Uh huh, and he deserved it. It still wasn't good for him. Now, shut up and get phoning before I get maudlin."

We worked our way through the lists of dive shops up and down the coast with no success. Finally, I started phoning large sport warehouses, the kind that didn't specialize in any one sport but brought in shiploads of merchandise to sell off cheap in giant one-time-only sales. On the fourth call I hit pay dirt. Oceanside Water Sport Warehouse dealt in all kinds of water sports and had held a monster sale of scuba tanks and sail boards the weekend before our dive weekend. Exhibit One's serial number matched one of the tanks they sold. The fellow on the phone couldn't remember anything about who bought the tank—two hundred and sixty-three tanks were sold in one weekend—but he invited me to come in and talk to the boss.

Janeen went home to catch some sleep finally, and I went back to my office to get the film I'd taken at the beach on the certification weekend. I also changed into my favorite rose-colored shirt and charcoal business suit. I wasn't sure how helpful Oceanside Water Sports staff would be. I wanted to impress the manager with my professional look before I tried to milk him for information.

I took the film to my regular one-hour developer and paced until it came off the machine. The first picture was a clear photo of the whole class. I grabbed it promising to come back for the rest, and roared off toward Oceanside.

Bill Carlyle, the manager, was quietly but enthusiastically convincing two middle-aged men that they'd find windsurfing a perfect sport for their fifties. "Silent, scenic, and it'll strengthen your upper body too. Builds muscle tone," I heard him tell the portlier of the two. Of course, it may rip your arms out of your shoulders first, I thought, remembering my first day on a sailboard. But whether it was the silent scenic splendor or the muscles that clinched the deal, the customers bought two matching Windsurfer Sports with sunburst sails. It took half an hour to finish all the paperwork, and good old Bill had to see to everything personally. My shoulders were rigid with impatience by the time he turned his attention to me.

"Hi," I said briskly. "I'm Cal Meredith, detective." I flashed my license at him quickly, hoping he wouldn't notice it was private, not police, ID. "We have reason to believe that a scuba tank sold by your store was involved in a death recently. I'd like to talk to you about it."

"You bet," smiled Bill. "We always cooperate with this sort of thing. Come up to my office."

We climbed a set of back stairs into a kind of mezzanine that looked out over the main sales area.

"Now how can I help?"

"The tank was serial number P225123, Dacor aluminum, eighty cubic feet, blue finish."

Bill rattled the numbers into his computer. "Yep, that was one of ours. We sold it the big sale weekend."

"Good. So do you have a record of who you sold it to?"

"No. We would only have that if they paid with cheque or credit card. This one must have been bought with cash."

"That makes things very difficult," I said, hoping he'd suggest something to ease the difficulty. But he only shrugged. "Okay," I went on, "I have a photo here. I'd like you to look at it and see if any of these people might have bought the tank."

"Look, Detective Meredith, we can get a thousand people

here on a good day...."

"Do your best." I gave him the snapshot. "All I need to know is if you recognize a face."

"What do you know," he laughed. "Pete Demchuk."

"He bought the tank?" I asked.

"Nah, I haven't seen that crazy boy for years. But you know what?— I think the blonde woman did."

"Which blonde woman?"

"The one with the cute spiked hairdo."He pointed at Sally and my heart sank. Still, it wasn't Jay.

"You're sure?" I asked.

"Sure. I remember her now. Right before closing that Saturday, she rushed in like her life depended on getting this tank. Made a big deal about it being a secret—she was getting it for her husband's birthday she said. She paid cash, wouldn't even sign her name to our mailing list. Quite a character—and that hair, I just wanted to touch it to see if it felt as thick as it looked.

That's Sally all right, I thought. I was going to have to go at her again after all. "What about Pete Demchuk? How do you know him?"

"That kid has haunted this place since he was eleven, buying gear bit by bit, begging for jobs, floor sweeping, heaving boxes around, anything to get money for scuba gear. He's got an obsession about dolphins."

"I've noticed he's pretty keen about them."

"Keen? He's crazy. One year—he was about sixteen—he made us a deal that he'd do all our mechanical trouble-shooting for a full year if we'd give him free scuba lessons. The kid's a mechanical genius, you know. Used to fix our compressor when the guys from the manufacturer couldn't tell us sweet tweet about it. He'd listen to it, sit there and cock an ear to it like a dog, and then start messing around with his screwdrivers."

"Hold everything. You gave Pete Demchuk scuba lessons, like open water lessons?"

"About five years ago."

"And did he pass?"

"Of course. He's a great diver."

"The little bastard," I thought out loud. "I wonder why he was taking the course then?"

"A regular scuba course?"

"Open Water Diver."

"Who knows? He certainly was already certified. But like I said, the kid's a nutcase."

"And he used to fix your compressor?"

"He sure did. Amazing kid, you know. He's got the determination of a bull moose in rut."

"That's a great help, "I said. "Gives me a whole new angle to concentrate on."

"Any time. Are you interested in any sports equipment? I can get you, or the force, a deal on anything you want—if I have the lead time, of course."

I smiled my refusal and escaped from the store. I thought about going right over to confront Sally with the tank information. But my heart wasn't in it. Besides, this info about Pete needed a close look. Maybe he and Ginny were closer than I'd thought. I'd get something to eat—I suspected raw cashews were the only edible thing in my apartment—then head out to see them.

I ordered a spinach pie at my favorite Greek hole-in-the-wall, and phoned for messages. The first call was Eva. "I've got you permission to see Jay this afternoon if you can make it by four. I told them we were working on an appeal and you're my assistant. That means you'll get to see her in an interview room, not in the public room with the Plexi-glass barrier and the telephones to talk through. But listen, in some of those rooms they have a two-way mirror, for the lawyer's protection, they say. So be careful. Don't touch her and don't say anything that will make them think you are anything but her lawyer, or my reputation is mud. Good luck."

I glanced at my watch. It was twenty to four. The drive to

the correctional institution was about twenty-five minutes if the lights were with you. I dropped a five on the table and ran for the Mini, without my spinach pie. It was one minute to four when I pulled into the prison parking lot.

After a cursory look through my official-looking brief-case, one of the matrons escorted me down a nauseatingly pink corridor to a series of small rooms. "You haven't been out to us before, have you, Ms. Meredith?" said the matron. "We just had the building repainted. They say pink makes people less violent. Cheery, isn't it?"

"Not at all what I'd imagined," I choked.

"No. People have no idea how hard we try to make things nice for our girls. Would you like a tour after?"

"Thanks, not this time. I'm running on a tight timetable."

"Another time then. Just settle down in there. I'll get Campbell for you. And don't worry, if you need help, just press that buzzer. We'll be right there."

I sat down on the chair indicated behind the desk. The interview room was small, filled by the one gray metal desk and two matching chairs. No non-violent pink here. I fought to keep from throwing up.

It was fifteen minutes before the cheerful matron returned. "I'm very sorry, Ms Meredith, Campbell says she doesn't want to talk to anyone. We don't force them to talk to visitors, you know. Not even their lawyers."

"But...but she *has* to talk to me."

"No, she doesn't."

"But," I felt confused. "Did you tell her who it is? I mean my name as well as the fact that I'm her lawyer?"

"Yes. She said she doesn't want to see anyone."

"Look, can you ask her again? Tell her we have some important new evidence that could have a significant impact in getting a new trial. Tell her I have to check some details with her. It's crucial."

"I'll certainly try." She smiled. "Some of them get quite withdrawn the first while, you know. I'm sure it's nothing personal."

I didn't want to pace. The two-way mirror was obvious, but I've never sat through a longer ten minutes. This time the interview room door opened, and the matron, propelling Jay with a proprietary hand on her arm, pushed her to the chair and forced her down.

I sucked in a quick breath. The blue denim work shirt and jeans she was wearing were at least two sizes too big. Her runners were obviously too big too, and without laces, they slapped the floor as she walked. But most shocking was her hair. Her incredible blonde hair had been cut in ragged clumps, between one and two inches long, all over her head.

"I cut it myself," Jay mumbled without raising her face to look at me.

"Why?"

"Why not?"

"But Jay...."

"When you come in here, they do this delousing thing. Part of the ritual. Doesn't matter if you have lice or not. They smear your hair with this vile cream you have to leave on for twelve hours before showering. I couldn't stand it. I was in the nurse's office being examined when she had to go to an emergency. So I took her bandage scissors and cut it off. I would have cut it all off if she hadn't come back and caught me."

"I...I bet that made you popular," I said, trying to regain a trace of calm.

"They put me in solitary for twenty-four hours."

"I guess asking how you are is sort of beside the point, isn't it?"

"Yeah."

"We're making progress, Jay. We found an extra tank and—"

"I don't want to hear about it."

"Okay, not until we have everything sewn up. I can understand that. I have one important question though."

"I don't want you to come here anymore."

"What?"

"I don't want you to come anymore."

"But Jay, I want to support you. I..." I glanced at the mirrored wall.

"Yeah, they're out there. All the time, watching."

"Jay, we're working as hard as we can to get you out."

"For fuck sake, can't you understand? I don't want to hear about it. I don't want to see you."

"If it's that important, explain why, and I'll go."

"Because every inch of you radiates everything I've lost. Every step you take is free. Every step I take is pushed by that insufferable woman, and I want to kill her. I don't know who I'll be by the time I get out of here. And you might not like the changes—I can see that on your face already."

"That's not true. I'm a bit shocked, but I..." I stopped, wondering if those shadowy figures outside the mirror could hear me.

"Just forget about me, Cal. I'm a killer, not a normal human being. And I'm getting the punishment I deserve. I've forfeited all my choices except to ask you not to come back. It's too damn painful, Cal."

"Okay," I said, working hard to keep the emotion out of my voice. My head was whirling. I felt like I could faint for the first time in my life, but I managed to push the buzzer that called the matron. "I'll only come back when I can take you home with me."

Chapter Fifteen

I was speeding up the island highway before my mind clicked back into consciousness. It was 5:38 though it seemed that years had passed since I'd arrived at the prison at 4:00. I was determined not to cry, not to give way to the storm of emotions I could feel whirling just under the surface. Eva had tried to warn me, but of course, I knew better. I'd insisted on seeing Jay right away. Now all I could do was redouble my efforts to get her out. And that was going to take a clear mind.

I glanced at my watch again. 5:45. I could make it to the 6:30 ferry and go to Faith's. Maybe a break would help. I turned the Mini toward the ferry terminal and floored the accelerator.

Faith welcomed me without question and poured the Remy Martin before saying more than 'hello'. I let myself sink into the chesterfield and savor the warm aroma of the cognac.

"So the investigation isn't going well," Faith said finally.

"It's okay, I've got lots of leads. It's just a matter of following them."

"Why are you here then? You look like disaster's struck, not like someone in the midst of an okay investigation."

"I went to see Jay."

"And she's not okay."

"No," I said and told Faith about our meeting. "She's obviously working very hard to be tough. You should have seen her,

Faith. With her hair so short, you really see those eyes and high cheekbones. She's unbelievably beautiful, but such anguish in her eyes. She only looked at me once the whole time and it took my breath away. And she had her jaw and her fists clenched up so tight, I could see the white of her bones. I guess being reminded of the outside is painful, but I...."

"You wanted to help her and you can't."

"Yeah, my white knight routine is remarkably rusted."

"She might manage, Calliope. Remember she's physically strong. Nobody's going to push her around in there. What she has to do is find her emotional strength. But I'm afraid it sounds as if she's totally accepted the institution's view of her, and that's very worrying."

"Exactly. It's like she wants as much punishment as she can get."

"It's the guilt about Tekla coming out again, I'm afraid. What you have to do—for yourself as well as for her—is concentrate on Tekla's death. Tell me what you've got."

I took a deep breath. Faith's no-nonsense assessment of situations always helped, especially when my heart started getting in the way of my brain. "Eva says I have to have motive, means, and murderer for the Crown. I have more than enough motive. Nazki has the strongest. His mother swore revenge against Tekla's family. Sally also had reason to hate Tekla and want him dead, but I don't want to think it might be Sally. She has some problems, but she has helped me with the Ethiopian angle."

"You can't ignore her motives just because she's a lesbian. We're just as capable of being murderous as anyone else."

"Ralph Dale hated Tekla, but his motive has to do with Ginny and he could have solved the problems in other ways. I don't think Ginny had a motive. She seems to have been crazy about Tekla although if he treated her like he did Sally, it's still a possibility."

"Lovers and spouses are at the highest risk to kill each

other, remember. Statistically, Ginny can't be ruled out."

"True. I need to spend some more time with her. There's some reason to think she was pregnant, and that would change things, though I'm not sure how. As for means, Sally has the most obvious means with the tank. And then there's Pete Demchuk. He seems to have been out to get Jay, not Tekla, but he still could have done the monoxide thing, with his mechanical know-how of the compressor. That still leaves the question of how the tank got to Tekla. As buddy, Nazki would have the best access."

"So you have to eliminate suspects. If I were you, I'd look at the marriage first."

"So much for family values."

"Indeed. Almeda always used to say 'If you want to die of natural causes, move far away from family and friends.' "

"And looking more closely at Ginny and her father, as well as checking on Peter, will give me a rounded out picture of everyone before I try confronting Nazki or Sally."

"Good," said Faith, pouring another shot of cognac into both our snifters. "You can catch the 6:30 a.m. ferry back to Victoria tomorrow and get started. And you can save me a trip. I've got these papers ready for Eva to finish the sale of the dive shop. You can drop them off at her office for me. Janeen will be taking over full-time next week.

"Now off to bed with you. The cognac will ensure a good sleep so you'll be fresh tomorrow."

* * *

I drove straight from the ferry to the co-op and had the manager buzz Pete. He was in his room studying and invited me up.

"Guess what?" he said. "I got the job with The Dolphin Project. I start as soon as exams are over."

"What job?"

"The diving job," he stopped abruptly and blushed.

"You mean you got Jay's job as chief diver for the

Project?"

"Yeah. I guess you think that's rotten."

"It's a bit opportunistic. You certainly have benefited from this little accident, haven't you? You got the job you wanted and you have a chance to get the girl you wanted. How convenient."

"Yeah. Funny how life works out, isn't it."

"Real funny. I'm surprised they took you when you haven't even got your dive certification," I snarled sarcastically, "since we didn't finish on the weekend."

"Uh, yeah. They...they said they'd help me finish up."

"How very odd. I would think they'd want somebody with lots of dive experience to replace Jay. Maybe somebody who could do other things too, like run a compressor, fix things."

"Oh I can fix...." Pete stopped and blushed again.

"You can fix things? Compressors and tanks maybe?"

"I guess I could."

"I hear you're very good at it. And that you got your diver's certification when you were sixteen, five years ago. Is that what it says on the resume you gave The Dolphin Project?"

Pete got up from his desk and paced around the room. I sat still and silent. A long uncomfortable silence is a most useful interrogation tool.

"I had to do what I did. It was absolutely necessary," he said finally.

"Tell me," I ordered and waited.

"The Dolphin Project is crucial to the world's survival. I've been out there and talked to those dolphins. And they tell me what needs to be done to save the world. The first thing was for me to get a job with The Dolphin Project so I could be with them every day. Jay ran their only diving program. So the dolphins told me I had to get a job with her or neutralize her. Since I'd heard she wouldn't hire anyone, I figured the best way was to pretend I was a new diver, take her classes, and get her to fall in love with me. Then she'd hire me. And if she didn't I could find out enough about her to discredit her. There's always something ugly in humans."

I stared at him. There was nothing in his manner that suggested he was joking or even exaggerating. He appeared perfectly calm and serious, as if this was the most normal conversation in the world.

"How do the dolphins communicate with you?" I asked carefully.

"Haven't you heard the tapes of dolphin talk?"

"I have. But I don't understand it."

"Most people don't. They only want a very few of us who they know they can trust. Human beings haven't been very good to them. I've made some tapes of my own. Do you want to hear them?"

"Sure."

Pete opened a closet which revealed hundreds of carefully labeled cassette tapes and a sophisticated stereo system. He selected a cassette and placed it in the tape deck. "In this one, we were talking about the tuna fishermen. They had a plan to destroy some tuna boats, just two or three, enough to scare the others off. There are hundreds of dolphins getting caught in those nets. I advised them to wait and let public opinion work. If they start sinking tuna boats, the humans will turn on them."

I listened as the familiar squeals and whistles of dolphin pods filled the room. "How do you know what they're saying?"

"It's obvious. Just listen. That one, he's lost two brothers to the tuna nets."

"I guess I'm not one of their chosen communicators," I said. "So tell me what you did to the compressor."

"Nothing. I could have. But when Jay drank all that vodka, I figured I didn't need to do anything else. Either she'd take me to her bed or I could report her to the instructors' association and get her disciplined for being drunk and endangering her students. The Dolphin Project guys would be horrified, and I could rush in and get the job. Turns out it worked even better than that."

"I beg your pardon?" I barely kept my tone civil. "A man has been killed and a woman sent to jail, and you say that worked better?"

"We have to reduce the human population. Tekla was no loss. And Jay didn't understand the dolphins. She had to be sacrificed."

"I see. How would you feel about telling this whole story to the police?"

"Why? I didn't do anything except pour a few drinks. I had nothing to do with Tekla's death. The dolphins made sure of that."

"And what about Ginny? Where did your romance with her fit in to all this?"

"She's a nice girl. She likes dolphins. I thought maybe I could teach her their language—until she made a fool of herself over Tekla. But my first mission is to save the dolphins. I couldn't worry about Ginny."

I got up. "Okay Pete, thanks for telling me all this. It clears up a few things I was wondering about. Good luck." I slipped quickly out the door past him, but forced myself not to run down the staircase. I could feel my heart pounding fast as it had been since he'd begun talking about the dolphins telling him what to do. I would have to talk to The Dolphin Project before the dolphins told him to do anything more serious. However, much as I wished otherwise, he looked to be out of the running for deliberately killing Tekla. But maybe not. It did seem that he'd go to any lengths if he thought it would help the dolphins. I decided I'd go and talk to Ginny and see just how crazy she thought Pete was.

It was only a half hour drive from the university to the Dales' neighborhood out in Metchosin, but it was worlds away culturally. The Dales' neighborhood was semirural, with little houses, often in a partially built condition, that told stories of people moving away from the city to find cheaper land and building their houses themselves. Not an affluent area, at least, not around Ralph's church and parsonage.

The parsonage sat beside the church, blind with all its drapes tightly closed. I pulled over, took a deep breath, and knocked on the door. Ginny answered.

"Why Calliope, how wonderful to see you. Come in. Dad and Mom have gone grocery shopping, but I can make you tea."

I followed Ginny into the kitchen and sat while she attempted, awkwardly, to find the teapot, tea, and cups. Obviously, Ginny didn't do this often. I sat quietly. Now that I looked at her I could see that Ginny's jeans were taut across the abdomen. No question, she was pregnant, perhaps as much as three or four months pregnant. So was this the motive? Was it Ralph, or maybe Ralph and Pete together? They did have a common interest in Ginny

"I was just over talking to Pete," I began. "He's excited about his job with The Dolphin Project."

"He loves dolphins."

"Yes. Do you know, he told me he can actually talk to them."

"Oh sure. He's been doing that for years. He says they talk about all sorts of things, even the daily news. I don't know how they could know much about the news. Maybe he tells them. Do you like your tea with sugar or milk?"

"Nothing thanks," I said. "Don't you think it's a bit odd that Pete can talk with the dolphins. I mean most of us can't."

"Why don't we go downstairs," said Ginny. "I've got my own apartment down there now that I'm married. Mom didn't think I should be living right in the family, you know. It's more comfortable down there."

I followed her down to a spartan but warm basement room. There was a bed, desk and chair in one corner, a rocker in the second, and a bar kitchen with a small fridge and hot plate along the inside wall. Beside the bed sat a baby's cradle decked out in pink and blue ribbons. Ginny plopped herself onto the bed and indicated I should take the rocker.

"You know," Ginny confided, "I do think Peter was a bit overdone about those dolphins. Just between you and me, Cal, I stopped going out with him because I thought he was going a bit crazy about them, like he thought they were God or something. Besides I figured out that he'd rather talk to dolphins than to me. Not like Tekla; it was always just me he was interested in."

"You must be pleased that you're going to have Tekla's baby," I ventured.

"Thrilled," Ginny said. "It's the best thing that's ever happened to me. Look at this," she pointed to the cradle. "This was mine. Mom's refinished it and decorated it so it's all ready. I kind of like rocking it already." She gave it a push and the cradle squeaked back and forth. "I hope the baby doesn't mind the noise."

I fought back a number of comments about things the baby might mind more. "When did you find out that you were pregnant?"

"Just last week, after...after the accident. I thought it was the accident that was making me feel sick," she giggled. "But it was the baby."

This didn't make sense. Why would Tekla be asking Sally to do an abortion two weeks before our dive weekend if Ginny didn't know yet? Unless there was someone else? Or Ginny was lying. Or Sally.

I decided to try a guess. "Come on, Ginny. Sally told me about Tekla and the abortion, and that was planned long before the accident."

She looked shocked, then shrugged. "She made me promise I wouldn't tell anyone."

My heart sank. "That's all right. It's different now with Tekla dead and Jay in jail." I felt like I was walking in the dark.

"I suppose. I do really owe her a lot."

"Tell me about it."

"I thought you said Sally told you?"

"I want to hear it from your side."

"Well, we went in that Saturday morning—Tekla insisted it was the only thing to do, but I couldn't. After he left, I pleaded with Sally not to do the abortion, and she agreed. She just made me promise not to tell anyone. Then she told me how to act as if I'd been under anesthesia so it would look to Tekla like she'd really done it."

"What did you think would happen when it became obvious you were still pregnant?"

"Sally said Tekla would just have to accept it once the baby was there."

"Oh really. So here you are, a widow with a baby on the way, and living at home. I see you're wearing your wedding ring. I guess your Dad's accepted the marriage."

"He's still not very happy about it. But he says that it's better we married than committed fornication. Isn't it a lovely ring? See all the carved serpents. They were very important in Ethiopian mythology." She held out her hand, admiring the ring herself, then bent her head suddenly and cried. "I wish Tekla were here to see his baby."

The tearful breakdown had the effect of being staged, and I wondered, as I had in Pete's room, about how calculated Ginny's actions were. Nevertheless, I moved to the bed and put my arm around her to comfort her. This also enabled me to take her hand and examine the ring closely.

Just then Ralph Dale burst into the room, with Caroline Dale clacking after him in her spindly heels. "Virginia—" He halted for a second when he saw me. "May the heavens preserve us. Haven't you brought enough trouble on this house? Get your evil hands off my daughter," he said, and launched himself toward us so quickly that my arm came up to parry his blow before I was aware of moving. The blow was shockingly strong and I rocked back on the bed. He would certainly have knocked me out had he connected with my jaw. I dodged sideways and jumped away from the bed. Simultaneously, he knocked Ginny across the head and she sprawled onto the floor.

"Mr. Dale," I started."You've got no reason to be angry at your daughter."

"Don't tell me how I should be. I know evil when I see it in my home. I am the scythe of the Lord. I have warned you before," he ranted. "Now I will see that you are punished."

"Father," said Caroline Dale quietly. She slipped quickly around and inserted herself between me and her husband. "We don't need to worry. Virginia is a good girl. And this woman is going to leave now."

"Turn your back on evil or you will die like the sinners of Sodom and Gomorrah," he chanted, but more quietly. Clearly Caroline Dale was experienced at dealing with these situations.

"If you'd just go," Caroline said to me, "we'd all be much happier. Virginia's fine. I'll make sure of that." She moved enough to let me squeeze by without letting Ralph any closer.

I didn't wait to hear more. I ran up the stairs, out the back door, into the Mini, and raced for home without once looking back. Once in my apartment, I made a point of locking the door with both locks before I poured the last of the cognac Faith had sent for Jay and tried to settle down by listening to some Bach. It didn't help. I paced around the room for a while, checked the television but found only wrestling on the sports channel, and finally phoned Janeen.

"The world is full of crazies," I told her. "And I've seen more than my share today." I told her about Peter and his dolphins, and about the encounter with Ginny, Ralph, and Caroline. "He really scared me, Jan. I think he would kill someone he thought was evil without a second's hesitation. For a minute, I thought he might be going to try to kill me right there."

"Well, you know you aren't his kind of people. And you were actually touching his daughter when he came in."

"I was looking at her ring."

"Do you think he might try to make good on his threat to punish you, Cal?"

"No, that's silly. He just spooked me, I guess."

"You can come and spend the night with me at the Mercantile Building if you want a bodyguard. I could stuff his head in one of my toilets. That would show him evil if he wants to see it incarnate."

I started laughing in spite of myself. "Thanks Jan. I think I'll manage. But if he comes by, I know right where to send him. Listen, more seriously, will you come with me tomorrow?"

"Where?"

"I've pretty well eliminated Peter from my list of suspects. Ralph and maybe Ginny are still on there. She's going to have a baby that Tekla thought had been aborted. It would be convenient for her to have him out of the way. But I have to have another go-round with Nazki to see if I can either implicate or eliminate him once and for all. And I have to face Sally with the evidence of the tank. So far, she's the only one with a means, unless Pete, the compressor wizard, was involved."

"You bet I'll come. I'll take great pleasure at getting whoever it is."

Chapter Sixteen

I couldn't get comfortable and tossed fitfully back and forth across the queen-sized bed. Snatches of the day's conversations played and replayed through my mind. At times like this, I particularly loathed my obsessive personality. I kept seeing visions of Jay, of Tekla, even of poor frightened Ginny when her crazy father came in. I wandered into the office, tried to do some long delayed filing, even flipped through Saul Taratsky's album of jewelry designs. Finally, I threw on an old pair of jeans and sweatshirt. I might as well go and join Janeen. I had worked with her occasionally before when I was broke or insomniac. And after all the work she'd done on this case, she deserved a hand with those toilets.

It was just before I reached the Mini that the first blow hit the back of my head. I felt myself falling forward and reached for the door handle to try to stop my fall. But somehow I missed. I was on the pavement. Violent pain was exploding in my sides. I tried to roll over to see what was happening, but only rolled face first into water. I tried to breathe, but instead, choked on muddy water. Pain exploded behind my ear. It was so dark....

* * *

I struggled and groaned. There were heavy beams crushing me. No, they were serpents winding around my ribs. They were going to crush me. And then Jay and Liz.... The serpents would crush us all. I had to stop them. I raised my arm to fight back and woke. The pain was unbearable. I tried to shift my body to ease it but the effort started me coughing. I couldn't get air. I tried to call out, but the coughing increased, each cough sending shock waves of pain through my entire body. I was going to die if I couldn't call someone.

Then Sally was there, holding an oxygen mask over my face. "Breathe slowly and don't move, Cal. Or you'll probably pass out again. I can't give you any painkillers yet because you're concussed."

I concentrated on breathing for a few minutes, even though the serpents whirling through my dreams were now whirling through my mind. Maybe I had some answers now, then again, maybe it was just delirium from the pain.

After a few minutes, Sally removed the oxygen and sat down. "What happened?"

"Somebody tried to kill me," I said, though my voice came out in a pained whisper.

"I told you to come and clean toilets, damn it," Janeen said gruffly as she moved into my view. "It's a lot easier than this detective business. Do you think it was Ralph?"

"One of the Dales, for sure. Maybe more. How'd I get here?" I asked when I realized that this was definitely a hospital room.

"The cops were hassling some drunks in your parking lot and came across you lying by your car about five this morning," said Sally. "You were conscious, sort of, and asked for me. So here we are. Do you have any idea what happened out there?"

"Not really. I was going to join Jan, but someone jumped me when I came out to the Mini. They must have been at the entrance to Market Square and come up behind me. All I remember from then on is pain."

"They left a message," Jan said. "Somebody wrote *The Lord punishes the evil doers* in lipstick on your windshield. That sounds like Ralph."

I shuddered. The thought of all that rage stalking me was terrifying.

"Okay. Enough talking. You need to rest," announced Sally in her professional voice.

"No way. I've got things to do and questions to ask before I sleep," I said, trying for a bit of humor.

"You're staying where you are. Somebody seems to have taken a sledgehammer or some very hard boots to your rib cage. There may be a few ribs intact, but not enough to bother counting. Your right lung has been punctured and collapsed."

"I have to get up. Every minute I lie here is another minute Jay has to stay in that place. This attack just proves that there is a murderer out there, someone who thinks I'm getting close."

"And it'll be a successful murderer if you start wandering around in the state you're in," Sally said. "I absolutely forbid you to get out of that bed for at least a couple of days. We'll think about it then."

"You don't want the murder cleared up, Sally?" I asked.

"Don't be silly."

"She's not being silly," said Janeen. "You could have good reasons to want Cal sidelined."

"I thought we went through that already. I thought I'd been given a clean bill of morality," said Sally bitterly.

"Did someone ask you to buy the tank, Sally? Or was it all your own idea?" I asked.

"What are you talking about?"

I pulled myself farther up against the tilted hospital bed, trying to ignore the screaming pain in my chest. "The scuba tank you bought at Oceanside."

"I...it was my idea of course. What's that got to do with anything?"

"And did you fill it with the monoxide or did somebody else do that?"

"I don't know what you're talking about."

"Come on, Sally," said Janeen. "We know you bought the tank that killed Tekla. We've got a positive ID on you. So just tell us about it."

"But I didn't."

"I talked to the guy at Oceanside who sold it to you, Sally. He remembers you very clearly and your concern about secrecy."

"Yeah, of course. We talked about a lot of stuff. But Cal, I haven't picked up the tank yet."

"What?" I started with surprise and the pain twisted me down and out of breath. Sally again grabbed the oxygen line and pressed the mask down over my face.

"Breathe as slowly as you can," she ordered. "And lie still."

I worked at breathing for a few minutes and at trying to ignore the pain and dizziness I felt. I had to find out about Sally. I tried to move the mouthpiece, but she held it firmly. I watched her. She didn't look like she was intending to kill me.

"Lie still," she said again. "I'll tell you what I can about the tank if you'll just lie still. I saw the ads for Oceanside's big sale. It was a bit early; we hadn't done our certification yet, but it seemed like such a good deal. So I went down and bought a tank for Dani, for her birthday. It's not till the end of June, but...it was a very good deal. And we are intending to get all our own gear. I paid the guy cash and told him I wanted it totally secret so Dani wouldn't find out. I was going to pick it up just before her birthday. That's the story."

"So you must have a receipt or a tag or something that says you're going to come in and pick up a tank, right. You wouldn't just give them the money and walk away with no record, right?" said Janeen.

"Of course not."

"Then I think you and I had better leave Calliope here to rest and go find that receipt."

"No," said Sally. "I have patients to see. What the hell

difference does it make anyhow?"

I motioned for Sally to release the oxygen mask and this time she did. "Look, the tank that was full of carbon monoxide, the one that killed Tekla was bought at Oceanside during that sale. You bought a tank at Oceanside during the sale. You admit you often wished you could kill Tekla. There are some obvious conclusions."

"Oh god, I don't believe it." Sally sat back down on the bedside. "Maybe one of the others bought a tank at that sale too. Hundreds of people were there."

"It's possible," I said, thinking that there was a chance she was right.

"I want to see your receipt," Janeen repeated.

"Calliope, give me a break," said Sally. "If I'd killed Tekla, and I thought you were getting close to me, why would I be treating you now? You must believe me somewhere in your subconscious or you wouldn't have told the police to call me."

I tried a slow careful breath and succeeded in getting some air with only a little pain. "We have to see your receipt, Sally. You can understand that, can't you? And I'm not staying here while you two go hunting."

Sally closed her eyes and was silent for a long moment. "Okay," she said finally. "I'll phone my office and have them cancel my patients for today. I couldn't concentrate anyhow. And Cal, I'll discharge you if you stick to a wheelchair with an oxygen tank strapped on it, and only if Janeen can look after you. What do you say?"

"I say fine," said Janeen. "I'll keep her in the chair and make sure she's tucked in safe and sound before I go to work."

I tried not to show it, but I felt some relief. I knew I had to keep working on the case. By now, I'd narrowed my suspects to three, and I knew the order I had to see people in. But I wasn't sure what I could manage without help.

It took Sally an hour to arrange things and get ready to

escape the hospital. I hid my face as Janeen wheeled me out. There was something too vulnerable about sitting in a chair being pushed around while people watched. I hate that feeling. And I certainly didn't want my late night attackers to see me. If they were the Dales, I was hoping they thought I was dead, at least for now. If it was Sally…well, I could be in trouble.

I'd decided that I wanted to talk to Nazki first. My nightmare of the crushing serpents had clued me in to which of his comments was bothering me—that he had never seemed to accept that Tekla would marry Ginny, and now I was sure he was right. I needed to ask him about those serpents on the ring to verify my theory. But it took a lot of arguing to convince Sally and Jan to take me to the co-op, and to wait in the car while I talked to him. I didn't want an audience for this one.

Naz was sitting on the verandah knocking back a beer when Janeen wheeled me over and then helped me manage the stairs.

"You're not having a good time these days," he observed.

"Not very. But you know what that's like, don't you Naz?"

"What do you mean?"

I pulled the photocopied news photo out of my pocket. "I mean you've had some very hard times in your life."

Nazki's face twisted into a scowl. "No doubt someone has tried to kill you for interfering in their family life."

"No doubt," I agreed. "Now tell me about you and Tekla or I'll call the police now."

"For what? I may have wished him dead, but I did nothing."

"Don't make me puke. You were his diving buddy. You had a strong motive and the easiest access to his equipment. And I can bet you're a member of the ELF guerrillas. If nothing else, I can make enough noise to authorities to get your student visa lifted."

Nazki glared at me for a long time, but finally forced his grin back into place. "Okay, okay, but I'm telling you, I did nothing wrong. I was going to go to graduate school anyway. Our organization keeps very good records of the whereabouts of the remaining members of the Solomonic family. When they found Tekla in London, they arranged for me to go to the School of Economics too. It was a perfect cover, and he was too full of himself to wonder why I'd be his friend. All I had to do was watch him—and make certain he never returned to Ethiopia. But your friend managed that for me."

"Why were you using the evil eye against him?"

The grin turned nasty. "That was a personal thing. I hoped he would suffer the kind of constant fear my family knew—and, I thought maybe, just maybe, it might work. Who knows about these things?"

"How'd he get the stone on the dive?"

"I dropped it in front of a crevice, then backed away and shone my light as if to look inside. I had to try three times before he saw it, and then he was frantic."

"And you just watched him?"

"Exactly, he couldn't pick it up out of the silt. Finally, he managed to get his glove off and get it between his fingers. He'd been acting strange anyhow, sort of dozy, shaking his head as if it hurt. For a minute, I was going to drag him right over to Jay, and then...I remembered my little sister. Najilah stepped on a land mine when she was nine, four years after my father died. Her legs were blown off and there was no medicine for pain. I remembered her face as she died. So yes, I just watched him."

I gulped a bit, trying not to imagine the little sister's face, then forced myself to continue. "What happened then?"

"He was struggling to keep up. He acted like he was having trouble getting air, and finally pulled off his mask and swam toward shore. I carried the mask with me for a while— guess that's what Jay thought was him when she saw its bright green stripe bobbing along beside me. Too bad. But it was her duty to care for us, not mine. And eventually, I did tell her he'd disappeared."

"You bastard."

"You don't have this kind of battle in your country. You don't understand."

"I know," I said, hoping I never would understand fully such depths of hatred. Nazki's story did make sense though, especially of the time discrepancy. And if true, it probably technically let him off the hook. "What about Ginny's ring, Naz? Did you see it?"

"No."

"She says it was Tekla's grandmother's. It's made up of gold serpents winding around each other."

"So?"

"So, I was looking at some rings a jeweler has made for different groups, emphasizing their symbols, and it occurred to me that serpents were an odd symbol for the royal Christian family of Ethiopia. Isn't that true?"

Nazki looked at me with apparent new respect. "You're right. The Solomonic dynasty would never wear serpents; that's a pagan symbol. Lions maybe for the great Lion of Judah."

"That suggests to me that Ginny has made up the marriage story and bought her own ring? What do you think?"

"Could be. I never did believe Tekla would marry her— no matter what sort of trap she tried."

"And she would have staged the break-in of your room to make it understandable that the marriage certificate had disappeared."

Nazki laughed. "That would explain why nothing was really missing."

"Exactly. Now, I've got one more thing to ask, and it's really important. Do you remember anything about the suiting up that day? Did Tekla get his own tank? Did you help him into it or was it somebody else?"

Nazki stared into space for a minute. "I don't know when he got his tank, but Ginny was hanging all over him, helping him with his stuff. Remember, she didn't dive that day."

"Right." I thanked Nazki for his cooperation and headed gingerly back to the car. I was exhausted and my body hurt dreadfully, but the picture was becoming clearer. I had to keep at it now. If Ginny had made up her marriage and had noticed me staring at her ring, that would explain last night's attack.

Back in the car, I got no cheers when I announced that I had to pick up my photos at the one-hour developer. I'd been snapping film all through the weekend and if I were lucky, I'd have caught what I wanted. Finally, Sally agreed and wheeled the Jag off to the developer's. Jan insisted that Sally go for the pictures while she waited with me in the car.

"Why are you stalling?" she asked. "Let's see if she can come up with a claim stub."

"We will. But I'm following a theory. Ginny was terrified that her father would discover she was pregnant out of wedlock, and more terrified that she'd go to hell if she had an abortion. It would be a neat way out for her, don't you think, if she could make everyone believe she was a widow, not a fallen woman?"

"You think she faked the marriage?"

"I'm almost certain. But to do that, she needed Tekla dead."

It only took a few minutes once Sally brought back the photos for me to find one that showed what I wanted. Sure enough, Ginny was helping Tekla put on his tank. I gave myself a mental pat on the back. Ginny had the motive, and here was a picture of her helping him on with the tank that killed him. All I needed now was to figure out how she got that tank. A nasty little suspicion began to form that Ginny and Sally could have concocted the scheme while they were supposedly doing the abortion. Then I noticed the second class photo, the one I'd taken to include the Dales.

"I have to go back to Oceanside," I announced to Sally and Janeen.

"What, you want to take me in to see if they remember me in person?" Sally asked bitterly.

"Actually, I'm pursuing another theory entirely," I said, which was at least partly true.

"This is the last side trip," Sally said.

It didn't take me long to find Bill Carlyle once we got to Oceanside. Jan wheeled me in, and apparently, Bill saw me from his mezzanine office. He appeared at my side within a minute.

"Detective, what happened? You were fit as a fiddle when you were here before?" He boomed, apparently convinced that loudness would be cheering.

"Just a small accident." I waved it off. "It happens in my business."

"What can I do for you? Some weights maybe to keep your muscle bulk up while you're...uh...."

"No, just help with another photo. I'd like you to see if you recognize anyone besides the two you already identified."

"No trouble." I gave him the photo and he peered at it intently.

"Barclay," he shouted abruptly and loudly, causing both Jan and I to jump in surprise. For me, this was unpleasantly painful. "Sorry," he nodded to me as he noticed my wince. "Barclay, bring your glasses," he bellowed.

We waited five long minutes, and I felt less and less hopeful, but finally, an elderly bespectacled man shuffled up and handed his gold rimmed glasses to Bill.

"My father, Barclay Carlyle. I can't get him to quit the business."

"He needs me. I'm the brains, and the eyes in the family," chuckled the old man.

Bill nodded as he squinted at the photo through his father's gold-rimmed bifocals. "You know, I think I sold a tank to the woman in the heels. I couldn't swear to that, but I do remember a woman with absurd heels coming in for a tank for her son, no maybe for a daughter."

"This class certainly seems to have been good customers of yours," Jan said sarcastically.

"Not surprising, Jan," I countered. "This place was offering a huge sale on scuba tanks less than a week before all of these people were getting certified. It would be natural for any of them to go looking for a good deal. And remember, the Dales were buying equipment for Ginny."

"True," Jan agreed.

"And this gives Ginny both motive and means. I think we're getting somewhere."

"Don't abandon our suspect in the car. I still want to see her receipt," warned Jan.

"We'll go ahead as planned, unless I can confirm this theory first." I thanked Bill and Barclay, and Jan steered me back out to Sally and the waiting Jag. It wasn't a car designed for this kind of load. While I sank into the wonderful leather passenger seat, Jan strapped the wheelchair down in the trunk before climbing in to sit up on the back with her feet between Sally and me. Still, even with my aching ribs, it was fun zipping along in the open car, and for a minute, I felt like a teenager again, going to the beach with no responsibilities. Too bad. My responsibilities were staring me squarely in the face.

"Okay, next stop, the Dales' house," I announced.

"Not a chance," said Sally. "You've got the color of a corpse, and if you don't get some rest, you're going to be one."

"I have to talk to Ginny."

"No. And especially not at the Dales', for goodness sake."

"Sally's right," added Jan. "And besides, you should be sending the police to the Dales."

"I'll take you back to your place," said Sally, "or mine. Take your pick."

Dani was kneading mounds of brown bread dough when we finally got there. "What on earth happened to you?" she said when she saw me.

"Somebody tried to kill her," said Janeen. "The Dales, we think."

"Oh, so that was your early morning emergency?" Dani asked.

Sally nodded.

"So, let's get on with the search," said Jan.

"What search?"

Sally flinched. "Dani, there's more trouble. I bought you a scuba tank for your birthday, but I haven't picked it up yet. It was supposed to be a surprise. But it seems the tank that killed Tekla got bought at the same place on the same weekend. Understandably, Cal and Janeen want to see my receipt saying I can pick up the tank whenever I want to."

"Understandably," Dani muttered. She went back to pounding the dough, then turned back. "You seem to have a talent for doing the wrong thing at the wrong time. You'd better clear this up soon, Sally. I hate wondering if I'm in love with a murderer."

Sally bolted down the hallway. "Through there," she pointed. "My office."

I wanted to pass out when I saw it. The room was a filing nightmare. There were piles of papers, books, and filing folders everywhere, on the desk, the bookshelves, the floor, the chairs, even on the radiator.

"It's going to take a while," Sally apologized. "I keep everything. I wouldn't have thrown that away. But I'm not very organized. I've been working on a medical paper for a conference and I just leave everything else."

"You don't have it, do you?" Janeen said.

"Yes I do. But I don't know how long it will take me to find it."

"I don't believe you," said Janeen. "I think you're an

accomplished liar and con artist who's finally tripped up. What do you want to do, Cal?"

I fought for another breath. I'd been slipping into sleep while Sally and Jan argued. "I...I suppose we need to watch while Sally hunts." I started to gasp for air. I wanted to speak, but I couldn't get anything out. Sally had the oxygen mask over my face again.

"I'll hunt for it," Sally said. "But you have to lie down. I'll fix you up with the oxygen and everything. Jan can watch me. You're badly injured, Cal. I can't let you make yourself worse."

Chapter Seventeen

I don't know how long I slept, but I woke up feeling as though Sally's soft bed was going to suffocate me. I tried to escape, but the coughing started again. Then, thankfully, Janeen was at my side holding the oxygen mask. It wasn't so frightening now, welcome almost as I felt myself react to the life-giving oxygen. The coughing stopped and some of the pain subsided.

"You need some painkiller," Janeen said.

"I need to be alert."

"She has a receipt."

"Who?"

"Sally, remember. She has a receipt from Oceanside for the tank. It does say the tank will be picked up, but it's just a receipt, not a claim check.

"What does she say?"

"She's stopped saying anything for the last hour. Just gave me the receipt and curled up in her chair. Dani's still baking bread, and I've been sitting here waiting for you to wake up."

"I want to talk to Sally."

"You're stalling."

"I don't have proof of anything. Just a lot of theory. And Ginny's just as good a suspect. I need to use the phone though."

Janeen brought me a phone and left. I phoned Oceanside to check on their use of claim checks for pick up of gear. Then I phoned Ginny, and asked her a couple of direct questions about her wedding and the heirloom ring. When I made it clear that I'd figured it all out, she admitted the wedding was only in her mind and the ring a purchase from the local Global Village shop. She also confirmed that her mother had bought her a tank but that she hadn't used it that weekend.

I was ready to hang up when I thought of one more loose end. "Ginny, did you get your ear infection treated when you came back to Victoria?"

"No. It just went away."

"I thought it might have," I said, then started to cough.

"Are you all right, Cal?"

"Not really. Someone tried to kill me last night."

I heard her sudden intake of breath. "Oh, I'm so sorry," she wailed. "Mom and Dad were so mad at me for having you in here and letting you...touch me, that I...well, I had to tell them something...."

"What?!?"

"I told them...uh...you were trying to...seduce me, you know."

"Thanks a lot."

"They were out till early this morning, and when they came in, Mom put a whole load of laundry in the wash—like there was blood or something on their clothes. I was really worried about you."

I slammed down the phone. What a swell acquaintance Ginny was. At least, she'd explained the attack. Not that it really mattered at this point.

I gave up thinking about it and phoned Eva. When I told her about my recent trauma, she was suitably horrified and agreed to ask Mary if she could get a warrant to check the Dales' house for clothes with my blood on them. The current state of forensic science would let them pick up the traces even if Mrs. Dale's laundry was whiter than white.

Then Eva told me about Jay. Apparently, she'd been involved in a pushing match with some other prisoners, and when a matron tried to separate them, Jay attacked her and broke her nose. They'd put her in a so-called punitive segregation cell for an indefinite period, and she could face further criminal charges. The very thought of it struck with more pain than any broken ribs could. The prison was destroying her. I had to act, and I was afraid I knew exactly what I had to do.

Janeen returned a couple of minutes later with Sally. With that startling hair of hers, Sally always looked upbeat, but I could see the tension bunching around her jaw. Her eyes held the shine of tears as she sat down on the bed beside me.

"Cal, I have the receipt, but Janeen's decided that's not enough. So, now what?"

"You could confess," I suggested.

"Damn it, cut me some slack."

"I talked to Oceanside, and they say they always give people a claim check as well as a receipt, and wouldn't give out merchandise without it. So where is it?"

"In my room, somewhere."

"I'm sorry, Sally, but I can't believe you anymore."

"So, you really are going to accuse me of murder because I'm messy with my files?"

"You know there's more than that. Why didn't you tell me about Ginny's abortion?"

"I didn't do it. I mean…Where the hell…?"

"Ginny told me. I want to hear your version."

"Shit, Cal, I couldn't do it. She was so upset. Clearly, it was his idea."

"You thought maybe he wouldn't notice?"

"She came in hysterical. I promised her that I wouldn't do the abortion. I coached her on how to act when Tekla arrived back. I figured it would be too late when it became obvious that she was still pregnant."

"And you gave her the idea to pretend she was married?"

"No."

"She said you did."

"She's lying."

"I just talked to her on the phone, Sally. She said you gave her the idea and she admitted buying the ring the Monday morning she came back from the island after Tekla's death."

"You can't imagine how terrified she was. I didn't tell her to pretend she was married. I did tell her she could tell her father anything about her relationship with Tekla. He'd never speak to the guy."

"But that would work so much better if Tekla was dead, right?"

"That wasn't what I meant."

"Come on, Sally. It's obvious."

"Damn it, you'd do anything to get Jay out of jail, wouldn't you? Even frame me. You don't give a damn about me."

My fury about what was happening to Jay broke. I wanted to leap up and shake Sally. I wanted to push her face down into the bed and hear her scream with fear. But I was too sore. And stuck with a lot of conjecture and no proof of anything.

"Why the hell should I care about you? You've got the motive and the means, Sally. And you're the one with the black hole in your soul, wasn't that how you put it?"

"You have no evidence," she mumbled.

"Do you know what's happened to Jay now? She broke a guard's nose in a fight and is locked in solitary for the foreseeable future. Her whole life is being destroyed."

"Fuck," Sally exploded. "Why the hell didn't she appeal?"

"You know why. Her trial was fair if she did accidentally fill the tank with monoxide. But not if someone else did. I have to give them the murderer to get her out."

I pulled myself up in the bed despite the pain and swung my feet onto the floor. "I know you did it, Sally."

"No." She moved off the bed, fists at the ready, guarding herself.

"He would have ruined your career."

"No."

"And he would have driven you crazy with his demands for things like the abortion." I got up and began walking toward her.

"No, Cal. Leave me alone."

"As soon as Ginny and Tekla left your office, you went and bought the tank. Carlyle remembers you clearly, and the rush you were in at the end of that day. The abortion must have been your breaking point, was that it, Sally?" I tried to keep the shaking out of my voice and kept walking toward her until she'd backed up against the window. My head was whirling and it seemed harder and harder to breathe, but I kept on walking.

"Get back, get away from me," Sally screamed. "I'll hurt you. Get away." She pulled back her right fist and I meant to duck, but the effort was too much. Instead, I collapsed at her feet, and she still hadn't thrown her punch.

She dropped to her knees beside me instantly and began checking my pulse. Tears were streaming down her face, and her hand shook as she pulled the portable oxygen over and covered my nose and mouth with the mask. "I'm a doctor...I don't kill people," she sobbed. "I couldn't hit you. How fucking ironic."

I pushed the mask away from my face and she didn't resist. "Tell me about it." I ordered as sternly as I could.

"I filled the tank on the compressor at my mechanic's shop with the old Jag pumping exhaust into the air intake," she paused. "Then I hung around that morning until I could give Ginny the right tank to give to Tekla. I told her it was extra full so he'd get a long dive."

"That's why you diagnosed her with the phony ear infection. So she'd be free to help him?"

"That was just luck. But it helped. If she'd been his buddy that morning, she'd have told Jay instantly if something was wrong. Nazki's hostility made it easier. It'll still be hard for you to get proof of all this."

"I'll get it, Sally. It'll take time, but I'll get it." I watched her carefully. She didn't look murderous, just defeated. "It'll take time that won't help you and could kill Jay, or hurt her so much…."

"Stop talking about her. Fuck, I didn't want to hurt Jay. I couldn't believe it when they charged her. I was sure that rinky dink little hospital on the island would simply accept an accidental drowning. It happens all the time. I had to stop him. I had no choice….Oh god, I've screwed up so badly."

"It's time for you to stop, Sally."

"If I confess, it would mean Jay'd get out right away, wouldn't it?"

"Probably." She held out her hand and helped me back to the bed. She looked desperately sad now that she was giving up; I hated being the one to force the issue. "The sooner the better."

"I suppose I have no choice. I can't go on like this anyhow. One favor, Cal?"

"What?"

"I don't want to have to face Dani. Can we leave as if I'm just taking you back to the hospital, and then I'll…I'll go to the police."

"You're going to need your friends around you."

"No. Besides Dani is too…too ethical to support a murderer She's already forgiven me so much."

"Don't underestimate her," I said as I heard the floor-boards creak outside the room. Sally turned and saw Janeen and Dani standing in the door way.

"Dammit, you've been listening."

"Why the hell did you do it?" Dani asked.

"He had a file. All the clippings about the bribery and deportation. He said he'd take it to the Medical Association if I didn't do what he wanted. And then he started turning up at my office. He told the nurses it was for counseling, and sometimes it was. I tried to help him. He was such a little boy, scared in some ways."

"Some help," said Janeen.

"Damn it, I did try to help. But sometimes, he'd come in and....It was so strange. He was so confused. I got the feeling he actually liked me, and thought he was being romantic. Other times, it was like I was the incarnation of evil, like I was personally responsible for everything that had ever happened to his entire people. Sometimes he'd....I guess it wasn't rape. I never did object and he...like I said, he'd act like I was his girlfriend. He'd even bring flowers, and then he'd hit me so hard....You remember the time I told you I fell up the stairs, Dani....The night after he brought Ginny in, he hurt me so badly, I...I couldn't think anymore. I couldn't think of anything else but stopping him any way I could."

"My good lord," breathed Jan. "We'll help if we can, won't we Cal?"

Dani walked over to the bed and grabbed Sally by the shoulders. "What the hell goes wrong with you? Can't you think of something normal like asking me for help?"

"I'm sorry." Sally choked out.

"Damn it, Sally," Dani continued. "I spent my entire life working on being ethical, knowing right from wrong, never hurting anybody. But you, damn it...." She turned and walked out the door, then stopped and just leaned against the wall shaking her head.

* * *

We called Eva. She came and brought Mary, who seemed sympathetic, until she started reading Sally her rights. Sally screamed and bolted. It was as if the consequences of her confession hadn't occurred to her until that moment. Mary was knocked off balance at first, but within seconds had grabbed Sally and wrestled her onto the floor. She pulled Sally's arms behind her and locked them tight.

"No, oh no," Sally screamed hysterically. "Don't lock me up. You can't. Please let me go."

"Eva, call me backup. I want a wagon," said Mary.

"If you unlock her, she'll go with me, voluntarily, won't

you, Sally?" Eva countered.

"The hell with that. You saw her take off."

"She volunteered to come in and make a confession. Get the hell off her."

"Eva, she tried to run. If I let her up, and she goes, I'll take her down any way I have to. That's my job with murderers, remember."

"She was damn well protecting herself and other women," Dani shouted suddenly from the hallway. She forced her way back past Mary and sat down by Sally on the floor. She slipped one hand under Sally's head and began stroking her hair with the other. "I'll stay with you, Sal. We'll manage together whatever happens. Try to calm down, love." Dani turned back to Mary. "She really is claustrophobic. Why don't you take her statement here? I'll make sure she gets to court when she needs to."

Mary laughed. "Sorry. The criminal justice system doesn't have special rules for the claustrophobic." She paused. "But you might as well come with us. It might help her."

I found myself wishing Janeen would take me home. I didn't want to hear any more, and it kept getting harder to breathe. Usually I was happy when I found a culprit; this time, I felt sick that I'd turned her in. But there was Jay to think of.

Finally, Sally calmed down enough that Mary unlocked the cuffs. Dani threw Janeen the keys to the house and walked with Sally out to the waiting squad car. Eva stayed behind.

"What about Jay?" I asked.

"With the confession, there should be no problem—at least, not much," Eva said. "We'll have to deal with the assault on the matron, but maybe I can get that dropped under the circumstances. Lots of paperwork and red tape."

"Today?" I demanded.

"Cal, it's Sunday. I couldn't raise a judge today if I was the patron saint of justice. But I should be able to do something tomorrow."

"And Sally?" I asked.

"They'll lock her up tonight for sure. With luck they'll take her in front of a justice tomorrow."

"Can you do anything?"

"Not officially. I have a clear conflict of interest."

"Shit."

"But I'll go with her to the jail now. I have a friend I can call to represent her. They'll be questioning her for hours and they have to be satisfied with the confession before I can do anything for Jay. I'll do what I can."

Chapter Eighteen

It was three-thirty Monday afternoon before Eva arrived at my place. She looked about as haggard as I felt.

"What happened?" I asked.

"The worst was the ride in the squad car. She got hysterical again. Mary questioned her most of the night. Dani waited and went with her to court," Eva replied. "The judge remanded her into custody for thirty days for psychiatric observation."

"They think she's crazy?"

"Given her behavior last night, yes. And it's not a bad idea. Having some testimony about the extent of her mental confusion about Tekla will help. I talked to Dani after court today, and after hearing the whole story, I think there's a chance we can get her off. I phoned my friend, Alice, who does strictly criminal law and she says there've been some decisions lately about battered women killing their husbands that might be useful in this case. The courts have accepted what they call the battered woman syndrome as a defense to murder."

"I remember reading about that in the paper. What's the rationale?"

"It's complicated, but basically, they're stretching the self-defense argument. They say a woman who has been threatened and battered, and who fears continued 'grievous bodily harm' or death loses her ability to think rationally about ways to escape. So given that, they accept self-defense even though the physical act of killing may not have occurred during an actual assault. That's really what happened to Sally here. Alice says she might be able to stretch the defense to cover Sally's case."

"So what about Jay?"

"I've managed to move enough red tape to convince the prison system to release her today. They aren't going to charge her with the assault though I almost had to give my first born—if I had one—for that. We'll still have to attend a formal hearing and get a court order quashing the conviction, but in the meantime, she's free to start her life again."

We left my office with Eva pushing me in the damn wheelchair again since I felt weak as a sick kitten, and stopped at Jay's condo to get her some fresh clothes before speeding out to the prison.

"Remember," Eva warned as she wheeled me in, "this will be a shock for Jay, even though it's a good shock. Don't be too impatient if she doesn't react the way you expect."

For a change, I listened carefully. In fact, I was quite nervous about seeing Jay again. "As long as I can take her out of here today, I won't care what else happens," I said.

"It could take as much as an hour for me to sort through all the documents with the Warden. I phoned ahead from my office, so they should take you two to a private interview room this time, no two-way mirrors. You can help her get prepared to leave."

I waited twenty minutes this time before two matrons shoved Jay into the interview room. She was shackled, hand and foot.

"For god's sake, take those off her," I burst out.

"She's dangerous," said the taller of the two matrons.

"Get them off. She's not guilty of anything. She's being set free."

"I don't know anything about that," said the matron

179

stolidly.

"The hell you don't. We phoned ahead to the Warden. She agreed Jay would be ready to leave."

The taller matron pushed Jay down into the chair and flashed a small smirk to her partner. The second matron, who looked unaccountably like an Airedale terrier, marched over and unlocked Jay while the tall woman guarded the door. They left without another word.

Jay didn't raise her eyes from the floor, not even when the door snicked shut behind her.

"Jay," I started quietly, "it's all over. I've come to take you home."

She remained silent, as if she hadn't heard.

"Jay, listen to me. I've come to take you home."

"I attacked a matron," she choked out at last, still not looking up.

"I know. It's all right."

"No. You don't understand. I broke her nose. And I meant to. I'm really violent."

"You're not violent. This is a violent place and it's hurt you. But you're okay. And we're going to take you home with us. Your time in jail is over."

"I'm supposed to be in solitary. I shouldn't be talking to you."

I could hardly stand watching her confusion and pain. I wanted to leap up and hold her close. But I knew she needed time...and besides my ribs weren't sure they could stand any ambitious hugging.

"You're not spending any more time in solitary, my love."

"Thank you for coming back, Cal. I was afraid you never would after what I said."

"It's okay. I'm here now. Why don't you come over here beside me?"

"I can't."

"Listen to me. You're going to be free. We found the murderer. You can come home today."

"Today?" Jay finally raised her head and looked at me. "Wait a minute, you're in a wheelchair. What happened?" She got up then, casting a quick look back at the door, and came over to me.

"Small battle with the Dales. I'll be fine in a couple of weeks, like new, the doctors promise."

"Damn it, I'll kill them when I get out of here."

"Please don't," I said lightly, trying to make a joke. "I'm fine, and I'll be even better with you out of here today."

Jay took my hands and held them to her cheeks. "I swear Cal, I won't let anyone hurt you ever again."

"Darling, all I care about is having you home safely. You don't have to become my bodyguard."

"But Cal...I still don't understand. Why are they letting me out?"

"Listen, love, Sally killed Tekla. She's confessed. You had nothing to do with Tekla's death, nothing, Jay."

Jay's eyes brightened for the first time. "Are you sure?"

"Absolutely."

"Thank god, oh thank god, I thought it was all my fault. I couldn't bear thinking I'd killed him."

"You couldn't have saved him."

"Oh thank you Cal, thank you for finding that out."

"Now listen, Eva's upstairs at the office getting all the papers signed. We're going home right away."

"Are you sure? Even after the matron...."

"Yes. There are no new charges. You're free. I brought you some clothes to wear. They're in the bag hanging behind this damn chair."

Jay took the bag, pulled out the royal blue silk shirt and pants that I'd chosen and held them next to her cheek. "My own clothes."

"Put them on. It's okay, we really are private in here this time."

Jay slipped into the silk clothes. It was clear she'd lost weight during the ordeal, but the soft material still hung gracefully on her, emphasizing her curves as well as her strength. I caught my breath. "You do look good in those," I whispered.

"Thanks."

"Now, the other thing I brought was my hair cutting shears. You know, I used to cut hair for all my friends in high school and for Liz. Would you let me finish your trim?"

Jay knelt down beside me and bent her head. I began running my fingers through her soft golden hair, massaging her head, touching each part of her skull, her neck, her shoulders, and finally her face. Then, slowly, I began to trim the ragged clumps. It didn't take long before Jay's face was circled with a soft blonde halo.

"There you are," I told her. "Sophisticated and elegant." I pulled my grandmother's silver mirror from the bag and held it for Jay. "Look, my love, see how beautiful you are."

Jay closed her eyes at first, then when I didn't move, she opened them and stared into the mirror for a long time. "I'm not the same person," she said finally.

"You look super. We'll leave here today and start a new life for both of us, together."

"Cal," she paused, "there's a lot of things you don't know about me. I…I don't want you to feel…well, stuck with me."

"Far from it. I know there are some changes and that's a bit scary, but we'll manage it together," I promised, taking Jay's hand and holding it with all the strength I could.

"I…I love you," she whispered.

"And I love you."

There didn't seem to be anything more to say then, so we sat silently, hand in hand, until Eva and the terrier-faced matron unlocked the door and entered.

"Ready?" said Eva.

"Yes, ready," Jay replied. She took hold of the wheelchair and began to push me out. The matron stuck out her hand as we passed. "Don't touch me," Jay snarled.

The matron laughed. "I was just going to congratulate

you, Campbell. You weren't fitting in very well here. I'm glad you're going."

Jay pushed on down the corridor without a word. Eva held open the heavy front gates of the prison building and helped lift me down the stairs. We were free.

Epilogue

It was two months before I could say that I was more or less recovered from the beating. It seems that inhaling mud puddles is bad for the lungs. I had, apparently, breathed in some decidedly nasty bacteria, so ended up with a major case of pneumonia to add to my injuries.

In fact, it took longer for me to get up and mobile than it took to immobilize my assailants. Mary had searched the Dale household and found plenty of evidence including Ralph's tire iron covered with my blood. Ralph and Caroline pled guilty to a charge of assault with a weapon, and the judge gave them each six months inside and two years probation, which was somewhat reassuring. It worried me though that they'd told their story to the local right wing tabloid which loudly proclaimed that they had acted to punish my sinful lifestyle. I wondered how many of their holier-than-me friends were planning to finish the job.

Sally's trial did not take long either. By then, Jay and I were staying with Faith for some rest and relaxation. I went down to listen the day of the trial.

Sally looked pale, and heavily tranquilized. Her face had a blankness to it that I'd never seen. Eva's lawyer friend, Alice, had made much ado in the local press about the battered woman syndrome, and let it be known that the country's foremost authority on the subject was coming to be a witness. As she suspected would happen, the Crown then came to her offering to reduce Sally's charge from murder one to manslaughter if Sally would plead guilty. Since Alice was not at all convinced that the battered woman defense would work for Sally, they took the manslaughter charge gladly.

I watched as the Judge jotted down notes before he spoke.

"Sally Arnot," said the Judge, "you have pleaded guilty to manslaughter. Do you have anything to say before I pronounce sentence?"

Sally struggled to her feet. She looked pale and frightened even through the drugs. "I...I'm sorry," she slurred with effort. "I already have a life sentence—waking up every day knowing that I killed him. I...I...." She collapsed back into her seat.

The judge nodded at the guards to leave her sitting, and seemed to turn his attention to those of us in the audience. "When I am called on to pass sentence, especially in a case as serious as this one, I must consider punishment, deterrence, protection of the public, and rehabilitation of the offender. In this case, given the obvious remorse of the offender, I don't think I need worry about protection of the public or rehabilitation. And given that the offender has been deprived of her license to practice medicine, I would say that she has already suffered some effective punishment. That leaves me with the matter of deterrence. While there is no minimum compulsory sentence for manslaughter, it is clear to me that to let this offender back into the community immediately would send a message across the land that a woman may kill a man with impunity if she can show he injured her at any time in the past. And while I sympathize with Ms. Arnot's very real problems, I will not be part of declaring open season on the males of the species. Therefore Sally Arnot..." He turned toward Sally and nodded for the guards to pull her back onto her feet. "...I sentence you to three years incarceration to be served in a federal penitentiary and I recommend strongly that you receive psychiatric treatment. Bailiff, remove the prisoner."

That night, Faith, Jay, and I went for a long walk by the ocean watching the sun sink darkly behind the neighboring island. As if to put a final period to the whole unhappy tale, we walked, for the first time since that April afternoon, along the beach where Tekla's death had occurred. Jay left us, walked to the water's edge, and stared out to sea for several minutes before she shook herself as if trying to shake off the past, then ran to catch up to us. She had begun to seem calmer here on Anemone Island than she had for weeks in town. Perhaps being in this close proximity to her beloved ocean as well as enjoying Faith's determined mothering was healing her at last.

I, on the other hand, was feeling pretty low. While I was pleased that Sally hadn't received a stiff sentence, I still felt that somehow she was more victim than criminal and shouldn't be going to jail at all. Meantime, I had no idea how Jay and I were going to pick up the threads of our lives. It would be a while before I was strong enough to go back to detecting. And as for Jay, she didn't seem to have any plans. She and Jan had fought like two dogs after the same bone at the dive shop on the only occasion when we had gone there.

Our walk took us a good three miles around the cove and it was dark by the time we got back to Faith's. She served up generous snifters of her ever present Remy Martin, threw a couple of logs into the wood stove, then began talking as if she'd been reading my mind while we walked.

"So, what plans have you two made?" she started.

Jay shrugged. "None yet. I guess we'll have to soon."

"I have a better idea," said Faith. "You both need time to recover from all this."

"Ain't it the truth," I replied lightly. "I rather fancied a couple of weeks vacation out of the hospital, but...well...."

"Money's in the way?" said Faith.

"Indeed," I laughed.

"A couple of weeks isn't enough either," she went on. "You need a solid period of time to get fit again, Calliope, and I know Jay needs some time to think about her future."

"Janeen's grapevine has been busy," Jay said.

Faith laughed, "I did hear that you and Jan don't see eye to eye about running the store," she admitted. "But that's all right. It helped me come to my decision. It's the perfect time for you two to take a long holiday together." She smiled, her magical face wrinkling into a wonderfully mischievous grin, and went to the mantel where she picked up a black portfolio. "Here are two plane tickets to Athens, two tickets to cruise the Greek Islands on the cruise ship *Maenad*, and a couple of thousand dollars so that you can pick an island and stay at least six months, more if you're careful."

I sat back flabbergasted, but Jay started laughing. "You're absolutely out of your mind," she laughed to Faith. "You can't just—"

"But I did," said Faith. "I know it's a bit highhanded, not asking you first. But I take the prerogative of being a crazy old woman, so I can do things that are for your own good. Besides, I know that for a long time Cal's been wanting to go and look at the archeological digs into the goddess civilizations. And I hear there's still some great diving in the Mediterranean."

"You can't do this, Faith," I said. "It's a grand gesture, but...."

"At my age, I get to make grand gestures."

After more discussion, liberally laced with cognac, Faith convinced Jay and me that her plan should be followed. We stumbled off to bed, wrapped in each other's arms and planning our cruise. We spent a moment pretending to waltz to a shipboard band, then for the first time since Jay had been released, we were making gentle, magical love. We made love for a long, long time, and it wasn't till the sun was already rising that I drifted off to sleep. I dreamed of dancing, hand in hand with a huge circle of goddesses, and woke up excited about the trip and ready to pack.

I never imagined this voyage to the goddesses would lead me into the most difficult struggle of my life.

Other Mysteries From New Victoria

IF LOOKS COULD KILL by Frances Lucas—Diana Mendoza, a Latina lesbian lawyer, is a scriptwriter for a hot new TV show featuring a woman detective. While on location in LA she meets blonde actress Lauren Lytch. When Lauren is accused of murdering her husband, Diana rushes to her defense and finds herself in the middle of a plot she didn't create. **$9.95**

TELL ME WHAT YOU LIKE by Kate Allen—Alison Kaine, lesbian cop, enters the world of leather-dykes when a woman is murdered at a Denver bar. Alison is fascinated yet wary of her attraction to a suspect, a dominatrix named Stacy. In this fast-paced, yet slyly humorous novel, Allen confronts the sensitive issues of S/M, queer-bashers and women-identified sex workers. **$9.95**

GIVE MY SECRETS BACK by Kate Allen—This second in the Alison Kaine series finds Alison investigating the death of a well known author of steamy lesbian romances who's just moved back to Denver when she is found dead in her bathtub—electrocuted by a vibrator. **$9.95**

I KNEW YOU WOULD CALL by Kate Allen—Phone psychic Marta Goicochea, along with her quirky cousin Mary Clare, investigates the murder of a client.
"Kate Allen presents issues facing the lesbian community with a humor and a humanity seldom seen in books today."—Bad Attitude **$10.95**

MURDER IS MATERIAL by Karen Saum—The third Brigid Donovan mystery (Murder is Relative and Murder is Germane) finds Brigid investigating the firey death of a self-styled Buddhist guru and the kidnapping of the young woman with whom he lived. Lured by the seductive Suzanne, Brigid gets caught in a tangled web of money, madness and murder. **$9.95**

NUN IN THE CLOSET by Joanna Michaels —Anne Hollis, the owner of a women's bar, is charged with manslaughter in the death of a nun. Insisting she's innocent, Anne appeals to probation officer Callie Sinclair for help. The case grows more complex and puzzling when another nun is murdered, and Callie discovers that sex and money are involved. **$9.95**

EVERYWHERE HOUSE by Jane Meyerding—The brutal stabbing of a philosophy professor implicates an angry member of the Furies, an ultra-radical lesbian collective. Student Terry Barber begins her own investigation, uncovering Barb's secret identity, a sinister religious cult, and growing political and personal struggles within her own lesbian collective, Everywhere House. **$9.95**

THE KALI CONNECTION by Claudia McKay—Lynn Evans, an investigative reporter, suspects the connection of a mysterious cult to possible drug trafficking. Her attraction to Marta, a charming and earnest devotee, challenges Lynn's skepticism and sparks her desire. Then Marta disappears. Lynn travels to Nepal to find some answers. **$9.95**

DEATHS OF JOCASTA by J.M. Redmann—What was the body of a woman doing in the basement of the Cort Clinic? Could Dr. Cordelia James really have performed the incompetent abortion that killed her? Micky Knight has to answer these questions before the police and the news media find their own convenient solution. "Knight is witty, irreverent and very sexy." **$9.95**

DEATH BY THE RIVERSIDE by J.M. Redmann—Detective Micky Knight finds herself slugging through thugs and slogging through swamps in an attempt to expose a dangerous drug ring. The investigation turns personal when her own well-hidden past is exposed. A fabulously sexual, all too fiercely independent lady dick. **$9.95**

Order from: New Victoria PO Box 27
Norwich VT, 05055 0027 1-800-326-5297
or buy from your favorite independent and feminist bookstore